James Allan Mair

The book of Scottish readings: In prose and verse

From the works of popular Scottish authors

James Allan Mair

The book of Scottish readings: In prose and verse
From the works of popular Scottish authors

ISBN/EAN: 9783337234010

Printed in Europe, USA, Canada, Australia, Japan

Cover: Foto ©Andreas Hilbeck / pixelio.de

More available books at **www.hansebooks.com**

THE BOOK

OF

COTTISH READINGS

IN PROSE AND VERSE

ROM THE WORKS OF POPULAR SCOTTISH AUTHORS

EDITED BY

JAMES ALLAN MAIR

EDITOR OF "THE BOOK OF MODERN SCOTCH ANECDOTES"

It is the chief glory of Scotsmen that, next to God and their parents, they
love their country and their countrymen."—BUCHON

SEVENTH EDITION.

GLASGOW AND LONDON

CAMERON AND FERGUSON

1888

PREFACE.

THIS volume needs but little by way of Preface. It may, however, be mentioned here that for its principal attractions the editor is indebted to the courtesy of many authors and publishers of copyright pieces, who, with a frankness he is only too happy to acknowledge, have given him permission to reprint in these pages a number of fine compositions which have not hitherto been accessible to the general reader. These pieces are distinguished throughout the volume by a note of acknowledgment appended to each. This and the other portions of the book will, it is hoped, present, within a very limited space, some of the choicest readings on Scottish subjects, in prose and verse, with which a spare half-hour may be beguiled.

It will be observed that, besides a variety of Poems, Stories, and Sketches in *English*, the Selection embraces specimens of the *Scottish* tongue in its old and also its more recent forms; and that the Highland, Lowland, and East-Coast dialects are well represented.

The author of "The Legend of St. Swithin" has (by apocryphal authority, he admits) translated the Saint from the Cathedral city of Winchester, to a temporary *Retreat* in the Roman Catholic seminary at Blairs, on the banks of the Dee, about six miles from Aberdeen. The localities named in the Legend have become well-known since Deeside has been chosen as the summer residence of Her Majesty the Queen and the Royal Family.

The illustration on the cover is copied by permission from a drawing by John Faed, Esq., R.S.A.

J. A. M.

NOTE TO SECOND EDITION.

IT was omitted to be stated in the First Edition that *The Execution of Montrose* appears here by permission of Messrs. Blackwood & Sons; and *From a Child's Diary*, by permission of the genial author, Dr. John Brown; and *Hail! Land of my Fathers*, with the cordial sanction of Professor Blackie.

J. A. M.

CONTENTS.

vi CONTENTS.

viii   CONTENTS.

THE
BOOK OF SCOTTISH READINGS.

SCOTLAND.

By Robert Chambers, LL.D.

Scotland! the land of all I love,
  The land of all that love me;
Land whose green sod my youth has trod,
  Whose sod shall lie above me.
Hail! country of the brave and good!
  Hail! land of song and story;
Land of the uncorrupted heart,
  Of ancient faith and glory!

Like mother's bosom o'er her child,
  Thy sky is glowing o'er me;
Like mother's ever-smiling face,
  Thy land lies bright before me.
Land of my home, my father's land,
  Land where my soul was nourished;
Land of anticipated joy,
  And all by memory cherished!

Oh, Scotland, through thy wide domain,
  What hill, or vale, or river,
But in this fond enthusiast heart
  Has found a place for ever!

Nay, hast thou but a glen or shaw,
　To shelter farm or sheiling,
That is not garnered fondly up
　Within its depths of feeling!

Adown thy hills run countless rills
　With noisy, ceaseless motion;
Their waters join the rivers broad,
　Those rivers join the ocean:
And many a sunny flowery brae,
　Where childhood plays and ponders,
Is freshened by the lightsome flood,
　As wimpling on it wanders.

Within thy long-descending vales,
　And on the lonely mountain,
How many wild spontaneous flowers
　Hang o'er each flood and fountain!
The glowing furze, the "bonnie broom,"
　The thistle, and the heather;
The blue-bell and the gowan fair,
　Which childhood loves to gather.

Oh, for that pipe of silver sound
　On which the shepherd lover,
In ancient days, breathed out his soul,
　Beneath the mountain's cover!
Oh, for that Great Lost Power of Song,
　So soft and melancholy,
To make thy every hill and dale
　Poetically holy!

And not alone each hill and dale,
　Fair as they are by nature,
But every town and tower of thine,
　And every lesser feature;
For where is there the spot of earth
　Within my contemplation,

But from some noble deed or thing
Has taken consecration!

Scotland! the land of all I love,
The land of all that love me;
Land whose green sod my youth has trod,
Whose sod shall lie above me.
Hail! country of the brave and good;
Hail! land of song and story;
Land of the uncorrupted heart,
Of ancient faith and glory!

By permission of Messrs. Chambers.

THE SCOT ABROAD.

WE were a merry party at the Heathermuir Lodge in the spring of 1854—for any prospect of active service is always welcome to young officers; and just at this time the proceedings respecting which Mr. Kinglake has recently refreshed our memories had reached such a pass that we all expected to be starting "Eastward, ho!" before many weeks were over. Hence, our gathering on the evening of which I speak might almost be considered in the light of a farewell entertainment; and it was proportionately jovial and noisy. Songs were sung, stories told, healths drunk, and cheers given in answer to them, till the glasses rattled on the table, and the very roof seemed to tremble over our heads.

Our host, Colonel Walter Parritchpat (who, though considerably past his eightieth year, made one of the merriest among us), was a fine specimen of what I will venture to call, in default of any better title, the cosmopolitan Scotchman. Entering upon active service at an age when other lads are usually still robbing orchards and wielding *bolster*-pistols, he had been successively a subaltern in the Turkish service, an officer of Sepoys in India, a farmer in Canada, an inspector of army stores at Vienna, a consul in Spain, and an attaché at St. Petersburg; and after all his wanderings, was still able to eat haggis or oatmeal-porridge with as keen a relish, dance a Highland reel with as nimble a foot, and chorus "Auld Lang Syne" with as much spirit, as though he had never even quitted the banks of the Clyde, where he was now once more snugly established.

One particularity of the Colonel's, which we all knew well, was, that his talk always came to its highest perfection towards the close of the evening. When he had a specially good story, or an unusually telling joke, it was sure to appear, like a kind of stirrup cup, just before the company separated; and consequently we all pricked up our ears when, after a long silence, he at last opened his mouth and spake,—

"Let me give you a word of advice, my boy," said he to Ensign Donovan (corrupted by the mess into "Downy Un"), who was very enthusiastic about our new destination, "don't expect too much from foreign parts, for they're very like parts that are *not* foreign after all."

Such an exordium, coming from the lips of a veteran traveller like the Colonel, made us all stare; but he proceeded without noticing our astonishment,—

"I knew a man once, now, who went abroad to find novelty, and, instead of that, found so much of what he had left at home that it fairly broke his heart."

"A story, a story!" shouted we with one voice, seeing

by the twinkle of the old gentleman's eye that something good was coming.

"Well, it *is* a story," said the Colonel, laughing; "and as it's rather early to break up yet, I don't mind if I tell it you. It was in the end of last century, more years ago than I like to calculate, that I found myself *en route* for the East, just as you youngsters are now, with about a dozen more scapegraces from almost every country of Europe.

"We were going to join the Turkish service, where hard knocks and high pay were to be got for the asking and of course we talked of nothing but cutting and slashing, capturing standards and winning endless glory, forgetting that we might be picked off by marsh-fever or cholera before we ever saw the enemy at all. The most enthusiastic of us all was an Englishman, a jolly, empty-headed, good-natured sort of fellow, who was going out as an interpreter, having somehow picked up a smattering of Turkish, though of Russian and the other languages of Eastern Europe he knew no more than I did. I found out by chance, before I fell in with him, that his ruling passion was an unquenchable hatred of everything Scotch; and so, just for the fun of the thing, I determined to pass myself off to him as an Englishman. Having been brought up in England, I succeeded very well; and to the others who were in the secret it was as good as a play to hear the fellow launching out against Scotland and the Scotch, never dreaming that his attentive listener was himself one of the hated race.

"I'm not going to inflict upon you the history of our journey up the country, which at the time I thought unendurable misery, though I know better what 'roughing it' really means by this time. Suffice it to say that, after several weeks of bad food, dirty quarters, days of crawling at a snail's pace along the worst roads in the world, and nights of being crawled over by creeping things innumerable, we at last found ourselves, with our trimness tarnished, and our ideas of 'glorious war' considerably modified, encamped at some unpronounceable place on the Lower Danube, with old Suvarov's grey-coats quartered within three miles of us."

"Did you ever see Suvarov?" asked Lieutenant M'Naughton (popularly known as "Lieutenant Make-a-note-on"), who was a kind of walking Biographie Universelle, and never lost a chance of learning fresh particulars respecting the food, drink, clothes, boots, and *tout ensemble* of any great historical celebrity.

"Only once," replied the Colonel; "but I haven't forgotten it yet. One day, when there was a truce for three or four hours, some of the Russian officers invited a few of ours to dine with them; and an old Bavarian cavalry officer, who was one of the elect, and with whom I had become quite intimate, thinking I might like to see the fun, took me along with him. We were all as thick as thieves in a twinkling, and there was a great handshaking and drinking of healths going on all round, when, all of a sudden, the hangings of the tent were flung back, and in rushed a little pug-nosed, dirty-faced fellow, dressed (or rather undressed) in a tattered pair of trousers, and a shirt that looked as if it hadn't been washed for a month—stuck his arms a-kimbo, and crew like a cock. I took him for a drunken camp-follower, and was rather astonished to see all the Russian officers start up and salute him, as if he had been the Empress

in person; but my old Bavarian, remarking my bewilder-
ment, whispered to me that this was Suvarov himself.
He chatted for a minute or two with his officers, and
then, looking hard at me (I suppose he thought I looked
rather greener than the rest, and wanted to give me a
start), asked in Russ, which one of the others interpreted
for me, 'How many stars are there in the sky?' * 'None
at present,' answered I in French; 'they only come out
at night!' The old fellow laughed when they repeated
what I had said, and told me I ought to have been a
Russian; and with that he bolted out as suddenly as he
had come in, and I never saw him again."

M'Naughton put up his pencil and note-book (which
had been busy during the whole of the last paragraph),
and looked round with the air of a virtuoso who has just
lighted upon an undeniable Galba, or a fragment of one
of the lost books of Livy.

"It was a few days after our glimpse of the enemy's
ménage," pursued the Colonel, "that the first taste of
retribution overtook my friend the Englishman. We
were strolling through the camp with a Turkish officer,
whose acquaintance we had made the day before, and
the interpreter was abusing the Scotch to his heart's
content, as usual, when to his utter astonishment (and to
mine too, for that matter), Hassan Bey turned upon him,
and broke out fiercely, 'I'll tell ye whaat, ma mon, gin
ye daur lowse yere tongue upon my country like thaat,
I'll gie ye a cloot on the lug that'll mak' it tingle fra this
till Hallowe'en!'

"You should have seen the Englishman's face; I think
I never saw a man really thunderstruck before. 'Why,

* This was one of Suvarov's favourite jokes.

good gracious!' stammered he at length, 'I thought you were a Turk!'

"'And sae I *am* a Turk the noo, ma braw chiel,' retorted the irate Glasgow Mussulman; 'and a better ane than *ye'll* ever mak', forbye; for ye ken nae mair o' their ways than my faither's auld leather breeks, that ne'er trawvelled further than jist frae Glasgae to Greenock, and back again; but when I gang hame (as I'll do or it's lang, if it be God's wull), I'll jist be Wully Forbes, son o' auld Daddy Forbes, o' the Gorbals, for a' that's come and gane!'

"At that moment, as if to add to the effect of this wonderful metamorphosis, a splendidly dressed Hungarian, whom I remembered to have seen among the Russian officers with whom we had dined, called out from the other bank of the stream that separated our outposts from the enemy's,—'Wully, mon, there's truce the noo for twa hours; jist come wi' me, and we'll hae a glass o' whusky thegither!'

"At this second miracle, the interpreter's face assumed a look of undefined apprehension, wonderful and edifying to behold—exactly the look of Molière's 'Malade Imaginaire' when he began to wonder whether there was really anything serious the matter with him.

"'Isn't that fellow a Hungarian?' said he in a low horror-stricken tone; 'what on earth makes him talk Scotch?'

"'Perhaps he's got a cold,' suggested I; 'but I must tell you that some of our savants hold a theory that Scotch was the original language, to which all nations will one day return; and this looks rather like it, doesn't it?'

"'Scotch the original language!' shrieked my companion; and breaking off in the middle of his sentence, he subsided into a silence more expressive than words.

"A few days after this, a scouting party of which I had the command took a Russian officer; and in order to cheer him up a bit under this misfortune, I asked him to dine with me, the party being completed by my friend the interpreter. Luckily our prisoner was a good hand at French, of which we both knew enough to go on with; so the conversation went smoothly enough, except that my Englishman, who thought no small beer of himself as a philologist, would keep bringing out scraps of what he imagined to be Russ, making the disconsolate captive grin like a foxtrap, whenever he thought no one was looking at him. At last, after we had drunk each other's healths all round, and finished what little wine we had, the Russian called upon me for a song; and as I didn't know any in Russ, I gave him a French one instead, which I had picked up on the voyage out. Then our interpreter followed on with an old Latin drinking song (which our new friend seemed perfectly to understand); and when he had finished, turned to the Russian and said very politely, 'Won't you oblige us with a song yourself? it ought to go all round.' The Russian bowed, leaned back a little, looked at us both with an undescribable grin, and burst forth in the purest native dialect with 'Auld Lang Syne.'

"'Bless my soul!' cried the agonized Englishman, starting up, 'is everybody on earth a Scotchman? Perhaps I'm one myself, without knowing it!' And thereupon, overwhelmed by this appalling idea, he slunk away to bed, where I heard him groaning dismally as long as I remained awake.

"From that day there was a marked change in my rollicking companion. All his former joviality disappeared, and a gloomy depression hung over him, broken by constant fits of nervous restlessness, as if he were in perpetual dread of the appearance of some Turkish, Austrian, Greek, or Tartar Scotchman. Indeed, what he had already seen was of itself quite sufficient to unsettle him, as you may imagine; but all this was a trifle to what was coming. For about this time our corps was detached to meet a Russian force under a certain General Tarasoff (of whom we had heard a good deal) who was threatening to fall upon our flank, or come round our rear, or do something else which he ought not, according to our view of the case. We fell in with the enemy sooner than we expected, and had some pretty sharp skirmishing with him for two or three weeks together; after which (as usually happens in a fight when both sides have had enough of it) an armistice was agreed upon, that the two generals might meet—to arrange, if I recollect aright, for an exchange of prisoners. After all the trouble Tarassoff had given us, and all that we had heard of him before, we were naturally rather anxious to see what he was like; so I and three or four more (among whom was his Excellency the Interpreter) contrived to be present at the place of meeting. We had to wait a good while before the great man made his appearance; but at last Tarassoff rode up, and the Pasha came forward to receive him. The Russian was a fine soldier-like figure, nearly six feet high, with a heavy cuirassier moustache, and a latent vigour betraying itself (as the 'physical force'

novelists say) in every line of his long muscular limbs.
Our Pasha was a short thick-set man, rather too round
and puffy in the face to be very dignified; but the quick
restless glance of his keen grey eye showed that he had
no want of energy. My friend the interpreter looked
admiringly at the pair as they approached each other,
and was just exclaiming, ' There, thank God, a real
Russian and a real Turk, and admirable specimens of
their race, too!' when suddenly General Tarassoff and
Ibrahim Pasha, after staring at each other for a moment,
burst forth simultaneously, ' Eh, Donald Cawmell, are *ye*
here?'—'Lord keep us, Sandy Robertson, can this be
you?'

" Involuntarily I glanced at the Englishman.

" ' I thought as much,' he said, with a calmness more
dreadful than any emotion. ' It's all over—flesh and
blood can bear it no longer. Turks, Russians, Hun-
garians, English—all Scotchmen! It's more than I can
bear—I shall go home !'

" ' Home !' echoed I in amazement; ' why, you've
hardly been out six months yet!'

" ' What of that!' groaned the victim, clutching his
forehead distractedly with both hands; ' there's nothing
left for me to do here. I came out as an interpreter;
but if all the nations of Europe talk nothing but Scotch,
what use can I be? I shall go home at once, before I
lose my senses altogether. I shall be talking Gaelic myself before long.'

" I never saw him again after his departure; but I have
since heard, that to the day of his death he remained
firmly convinced that the Turkish conquest at Constan-
tinople, and the subsequent rise of the Ottoman Empire,

were a malicious invention of historians, and that all the inhabitants of Eastern Europe were in reality Scotchmen in disguise."

A shout of applauding laughter greeted the conclusion of the Colonel's story; and it being now long past midnight, we dispersed to our respective apartments.—*By permission, from "Cassell's Magazine."*

THE EXECUTION OF MONTROSE.

BY PROFESSOR AYTOUN.

I.

COME hither, Evan Cameron!
    Come, stand beside my knee—
I hear the river roaring down
    Towards the wintry sea.
There's shouting on the mountain-side,
    There's war within the blast—
Old faces look upon me,
    Old forms go trooping past
I hear the pibroch wailing
    Amidst the din of fight,
And my dim spirit wakes again
    Upon the verge of night.

II.

'Twas I that led the Highland host
    Through wild Lochaber's snows,
What time the plaided clans came down
    To battle with Montrose.

I 've told thee how the Southrons fell
   Beneath the broad claymore,
And how we smote the Campbell clan
   By Inverlochy's shore.
I 've told thee how we swept Dundee,
   And tamed the Lindsays' pride;
But never have I told thee yet
   How the great Marquis died.

III.

A traitor sold him to his foes!
   Oh, deed of deathless shame!
I charge thee, boy, if e'er thou meet
   With one of Assynt's name—
Be it upon the mountain's side,
   Or yet within the glen,
Stand he in martial gear alone,
   Or backed by armèd men—
Face him, as thou would'st face the man
   Who wronged thy sire's renown;
Remember of what blood thou art,
   And strike the caitiff down!

IV.

They brought him to the Watergate,
   Hard bound with hempen span,
As though they held a lion there,
   And not a fenceless man.
They set him high upon a cart—
   The hangman rode below—
They drew his hands behind his back,
   And bared his noble brow.
Then, as a hound is slipped from leash,
   They cheered the common throng,
And blew the note with yell and shout,
   And bade him pass along.

V.

It would have made a brave man's heart
    Grow sad and sick that day,
To watch the keen malignant eyes
    Bent down on that array.
There stood the Whig west-country lords,
    In balcony and bow;
There sat their gaunt and withered dames,
    And their daughters all a-row.
And every open window
    Was full as full might be
With black-robed Covenanting carles,
    That goodly sport to see!

VI.

But when he came, though pale and wan,
    He looked so great and high,
So noble was his manly front,
    So calm his steadfast eye;
The rabble rout forbore to shout,
    And each man held his breath,
For well they knew the hero's soul
    Was face to face with death.
And then a mournful shudder
    Through all the people crept,
And some that came to scoff at him
    Now turned aside and wept.

VII.

But onwards—always onwards,
    In silence and in gloom,
The dreary pageant laboured,
    Till it reached the house of doom.
Then first a woman's voice was heard
    In jeer and laughter loud,
And an angry cry and a hiss arose
    From the heart of the tossing crowd:

Then, as the Græme looked upwards,
    He saw the ugly smile
Of him who sold his king for gold—
    The master-fiend Argyle !

                VIII.

The Marquis gazed a moment,
    And nothing did he say;
But the cheek of Argyle grew ghastly pale,
    And he turned his eyes away.
The painted harlot by his side,
    She shook through every limb,
For a roar like thunder swept the street,
    And hands were clenched at him ;
And a Saxon soldier cried aloud,
    " Back, coward, from thy place !
For seven long years thou hast not dared
    To look him in the face."

                IX.

Had I been there with sword in hand,
    And fifty Camerons by,
That day through high Dunedin's streets,
    Had pealed the slogan-cry.
Not all their troops of trampling horse,
    Nor might of mailèd men—
Not all the rebels in the south
    Had borne us backwards then !
Once more his foot on Highland heath
    Had trod as free as air,
Or I, and all who bore my name,
    Been laid around him there !

                X.

It might not be.   They placed him next
    Within the solemn hall,

Where once the Scottish kings were throned
　　Amidst their nobles all.
But there was dust of vulgar feet
　　On that polluted floor,
And perjured traitors filled the place
　　Where good men sate before.
With savage glee came Warristoun
　　To read the murderous doom ;
And then uprose the great Montrose,
　　In the middle of the room.

XI.

" Now, by my faith, as belted knight,
　　And by the name I bear,
And by the bright Saint Andrew's cross
　　That waves above us there—
Yea, by a greater, mightier oath—
　　And oh, that such should be !—
By that dark stream of royal blood
　　That lies 'twixt you and me—
I have not sought in battle-field
　　A wreath of such renown,
Nor dared I hope on my dying day
　　To win the martyr's crown !

XII.

" There is a chamber far away,
　　Where sleep the good and brave;
But a better place ye have named for me
　　Than by my father's grave.
For truth and right, 'gainst treason's might.
　　This hand hath always striven,
And ye raise it up for a witness still
　　In the eye of earth and heaven.
Then nail my head on yonder tower
　　Give every town a limb—
And God who made shall gather them:
　　I go from you to Him !"

XIII.

The morning dawned full darkly,
  The rain came flashing down,
And the jagged streak of the levin-bolt
  Lit up the gloomy town:
The thunder crashed across the heaven,
  The fatal hour was come ;
Yet aye broke in with muffled beat
  The 'larm of the drum.
There was madness on the earth below,
  And anger in the sky,
And young and old, and rich and poor,
  Came forth to see him die.

XIV.

Ah, God! that ghastly gibbet!
  How dismal 'tis to see
The great tall spectral skeleton,
  The ladder, and the tree!
Hark ! hark ! it is the clash of arms—
  The bells begin to toll—
" He is coming ! he is coming !
  God's mercy on his soul !"
One last long peal of thunder—
  The clouds are cleared away,
And the glorious sun once more looks down
  Amidst the dazzling day.

XV.

"He is coming ! he is coming!"
  Like a bridegroom from his room,
Came the hero from his prison
  To the scaffold and the doom.
There was glory on his forehead,
  There was lustre in his eye,
And he never walked to battle
  More proudly than to die;

There was colour in his visage,
  Though the cheeks of all were wan,
And they marvelled as they saw him pass,
  That great and goodly man !

XVI.

He mounted up the scaffold,
  And he turned him to the crowd ;
But they dared not trust the people,
  So he might not speak aloud.
But he looked upon the heavens,
  And they were clear and blue,
And in the liquid ether   .
  The eye of God shone through!
Yet a black and murky battlement
  Lay resting on the hill,
As though the thunder slept within—
  All else was calm and still.

XVII.

The grim Geneva ministers
  With anxious scowl drew near,
As you have seen the ravens flock
  Around the dying deer.
He would not deign them word nor sign,
  But alone he bent the knee,
And veiled his face for Christ's dear grace
  Beneath the gallows-tree.
Then radiant and serene he rose,
  And cast his cloak away:
For he had ta'en his latest look
  Of earth, and sun, and day.

XVIII.

A beam of light fell o 'er him,
  Like a glory round the shriven,

And he climbed the lofty ladder
  As it were the path to heaven.
Then came a flash from out the cloud
  And a stunning thunder-roll;
And no man dared to look aloft,
  For fear was on every soul.
There was another heavy sound,
  A hush, and then a groan ;
And darkness swept across the sky—
  The work of death was done!

  By permission of Messrs. Blackwood & Sons.

TIBBIELEERIE ON SCANDAL.*

By JAMES SMITH.

INDEED an' I'm sure it's perfectly astonishin' what folk in this world get to say aboot ane anither; for, oh! I hate scandal. Instead o' mindin' their ain affairs, their first and foremost desire's to ken what Lucky This, an' Lucky That's aboot—what they eat, what they drink, an' what they pit on—whaur they gaed to last nicht, an' whaur they're gaun the morn. I declare that, to a virtuous woman like me, wi' a weel-regulated mind, it's perfectly disgracefu'. There was nae less than yesterday, Mistress Pottyface gaed oot wi' a three-guinea plaid owre her puir bits o' skinny shouthers; an' I'm perfectly certain she never got that plaid in a guid way; for her man's

* By permission of the Author, from *Humorous Scotch Stories:* J. Menzies, & Co., Edinburgh.

naething but a porter in a tea shop, wi' ten shillings a week; an' I leave ony respectable person, wi' a virtuous, weel-regulated mind, to judge hoo *that* can be; but I hate scandal.

An' there's Lucky Sheepshank, the mangie-wife, that gaed awa for twa days to the sea-bathin'—'od help us! An' to be upsides wi' Mistress M'Funk, the pie-wife, she stuck up a big printed bill in her wundy:—" Bundles o' claes to be left next door!" I declare, when I heard it, I could dae naething but groan an' pech wi' indignation; for hooever ony woman wi' seven sma' bairns, an' a man oot o' wark, could gang awa for twa mortal days to the sea-bathin', I leave ony body wi' a virtuous, weel-regulated mind, to judge; but I hate scandal.

But it's very easily seen, after a'. She borrows frae a'body, an' pays naebody. But, by my word, when she cam back, she heard o't; for I gaed owre to her, an' says I, " Mistress Sheepshank, I'll thank ye to pay me the sixteenpence ye've borrowed frae me this last three weeks back in ha'p'nys an' pennies. It's weel for you that can gang to the sea-bathin' on ither folk's siller."

" I'll pay ye when I'm ready," says the madam, bridlin' up.

" Mistress Sheepshank," says I, " ye're an abominable twa-faced randy."

" I'll be the liker you, then," says she, an' banged tae the door in my face; an' that was the end o' my sixteen-pence—the impertinent, mean, low woman!

But I cried through the key-hole, " Bring back Mistress Maclaver's twa pinfu' o' claes ye couldna account for last week—*that's* yer sea-bathin', my leddy!" Oh, I had her there! She never cam oot a' that day. For it was

Mistress Maclaver hersel' that telt me; an' I could tell mair than a' that if I likit; but I hate scandal.

Weel, I gaed up the stair in sic a state wi' the nerves, that I thocht I wadna be the waur o' a wee drappie speerits; an' pittin' the bottle in my hand-basket, I gaed awa doon to John Blue, the grocer's, when wha should come in but Mistress Inquisitive for a bottle o' skeechin. Noo, Mistress Inquisitive's the disgrace o' the whole neighbourhood; for she aye maks 't her business to gang howkin' aboot ither folk's houses, an' likes to ken a' thing that 's gaun on; an' she keeps her wundy ever-lastingly open to hear what folk 's sayin', an' see what they 're daein'; although she pretends it 's the fine fresh air she 's sic a notion o', that she canna want it. But I was determined she wadna ken what *I* wanted; sae I says,—" Gie me a forpit o' yer best tatties, Maister Blue, for I'm in a hurry;" hoping she wad gang awa. But na: there she stood. At last she turned round an' said, in her usual mealy-mouthed manner :—" It 's a fine mornin', Tibbieleerie," lookin' slyly into my basket. "If you please, Mistress Inquisitive," says I, " I 'll be obleedged to ye if ye 'll tell that to the weather-clerk, an' mind yer ain affairs." Sae she gangs oot, an' says sae disdainfu' like,—" A forpit o' tatties—mphm!" wi' anither sly keek at my basket. " Skeechin to parritch! skeechin to par-ritch!" I cried back at her—the miserable, wizzen-faced-lookin' atomy. " Tatties—tatties—tatties!—" says she again—the impertinent, low woman.

But I can tell ae thing, an' that's no twa—Mistress Inquisitive 's a sly drinker. Her man 's a beggar-catcher; an' when he gangs oot at nicht, maybe I dinna ken wha sits up wi' her, hour after hour, owre fried sausages an'

C

warm porter and sugar. Oh no! I've nae business wi't; but hooever ony respectable woman can live at heck-an'-manger at nicht, an' bamboozle her puir simple man in the mornin' wi' skeechin to his parritch, I leave ony respectable person wi' a virtuous, weel-regulated mind to judge; but I hate scandal.

An' there's Mistress Greasypouches, her next-door neebour, that's no muckle better. She gies hersel' sic grand airs, an' no ae fardin to rub on anither. An' it's perfectly astonishin' hoo she can dress hersel' an her puir dowdies o' dochters like a wheen Frenchified dancin'-dalls, wi' bannits stickin' on the back o' their heids, trimmed wi' a' the colours o' creation, an' parysoles, 'od help us! an' unmercifu' big girrs roun' their bits o' petticoaties, lookin' for a' the world like a balloon in the last stage o' inflammation; an' as muckle hair on the back o' their heids, tae, that looks mair like a kist o' drawers than onything else.

There's *some* folk I could name that can tak' on frae this shop an' the ither shop, an' mak fine puir mouths when they're craved for siller. But it'll never be *me* that'll tell wha they are; for oh! I hate scandal.

As I said the ither day to Mistress Puddinface,— "What a blessed thing it is to ha'e a kind word to say o' folk's neebours." This was on the road comin' hame frae the market. "Ay," says she, lookin' me broad in the face, "it's very true." "An' what hae ye been buyin' the day, na?" says I, in my very mildest manner. "A rabbit," says she, tryin' to look very grand. "Oh, Mistress Puddinface!" says I, "hoo can ye tell sic a dounricht falsehood; as if I didna see ye buyin' a pennyworth o' banes wi' my ain een! Oh, woman,

woman, hoo can ye say 't?" I didna see 't, ye ken, but I
thocht it; an' it comes a' to the same thing. "There's
ae thing I ken *you'll* never buy," says she, wi' a spitefu'
girn. "An' what's that?" says I, in my very mildest
manner again. "A kind an' charitable word to say o'
folk's neebours," says she—the impertinent, low woman.
But that's aye the way that weel-meanin' folk's ta'en up
in a wrang licht. I could tell plenty about *her* tae, if I
likit; but I hate scandal.

I was served the very same way by Mistress Bletherer.
I had gane awa to my tea ae afternoon up to Miss Sugarploum's, wi' a new bannit that didna happen to be paid
for (but that's naebody's business). Sae, as I'm gaun
alang the street, wha does I see but Mistress Bletherer
an' Mistress Inquisitive stannin' at the well. An' when
they saw me, the tane says to the tither,—"Did ye ever
s̈ee sic a Death upon Spunks!" the low mean trash. But
I held up my tails like a duchess, an' never let on I
saw them. Sae I gaed to Miss Sugarploum's—the sweet
crater—an' had a very fine cup o' tea, an' some very nice
cordial mixed wi' speerits (but that's naebody's business).
Weel, when the cordial was finished, I bade her guid-
nicht; an' as I gaed doun the stair into the open air, I
felt a weakness in my legs that I couldna very weel
account for; but I held on till I reached the stairfit,
when that abominable woman, Mistress Bletherer, met
me on the stair, an' cried after me, at the highest pitch o'
her voice,—"Tibbieleerie's drunk! Tibbieleerie's drunk!"
the impertinent low woman, to tell *me* I was drunk,
when it was only a natural weakness in my puir legs!
But I can tell Mistress Bletherer that she had better tak'
care wha she's meddlin' wi'. She gangs oot on the

Sundays wi' a braw satin dress, an' a *veil* on, nae less; an' her man's naething but a puir tax-collector, wi' nine shillings a-week. He pretends to be very religious, tae, tho' it's weel kent he's a notorious hypocrite. He gaed the ither day to Tam Dunderhead's wi' a tract "for his comfort," as he ca'ed it; an' when Tam opened oot the paper, what was this but a Pavin' Board Tax for five-an'-ninepence! But it's weel kent hoo the satin dress comes. Oh, maybe there's nae siller kept up frae the proper authorities! Oh, maybe no!

That very next Sunday after she insulted me, an' just as I was preparin' for the kirk, I saw the madam frae the wundy, gaun sailin' oot, as usual; an' I up wi' the wundy, an' cries after her,—"There's Lucky Bletherer wi' the Pavin' Board Tax on her back!" My wordy! she got something to think on *that* day "for her comfort!"

But hooever ony woman can gang oot dressed like a duchess on nine shillings a-week, I leave ony respectable person wi' a virtuous, weel-regulated mind, to judge; but I never said an ill word against onybody in my life; an' let me tell ye, it's a grand consolation to think sae. For, oh! I hate scandal.

MARY QUEEN OF SCOTS.

By Henry Glassford Bell.

I LOOK'D far back into other years, and lo! in bright array,
I saw, as in a dream, the forms of ages passed away.

It was a stately convent, with its old and lofty walls,
And gardens, with their broad green walks, where soft the footstep
falls;

And o'er the antique dial-stone the creeping shadow pass'd,
And, all around, the noon-day sun a drowsy radiance cast.
No sound of busy life was heard, save from the cloister dim,
The tinkling of the silver bell, or the sisters' holy hymn.
And there five noble maidens sat, beneath the orchard trees,
In that first budding spring of youth, when all its prospects please.
And little reck'd they, when they sang, or knelt at vesper prayers,
That Scotland knew no prouder names—held none more dear than
    theirs;—
And little even the loveliest thought, before the Virgin's shrine,
Of royal blood, and high descent from the ancient Stuart line;
Calmly her happy days flew on, uncounted in their flight,
And, as they flew, they left behind a long-continuing light.

The scene was changed.   It was the court—the gay court of
    Bourbon:
And 'neath a thousand silver lamps, a thousand courtiers throng;
And proudly kindles Henry's eye—well pleased, I ween, to see
The land assemble all its wealth of grace and chivalry:—
Grey Montmorency, o'er whose head had pass'd a storm of years,
Strong in himself and children, stands the first among his peers;
And next the Guises, who so well fame's steepest heights assail'd,
And walk'd ambition's diamond ridge, where bravest hearts have
    fail'd;
And higher yet their path shall be, stronger shall wax their might,
For before them Montmorency's star shall pale its waning light.
Here Louis, Prince of Condé, wears his all unconquer'd sword,
With great Coligni by his side—each name a household word!
And there walks she of Medicis—that proud Italian line,
The mother of a race of kings—the haughty Catherine!
The forms that follow in her train, a glorious sunshine make—
A milky way of stars that grace a comet's glittering wake;
But fairer far than all the rest, who bask on fortune's tide,
Effulgent in the light of youth, is she, the new-made bride!
The homage of a thousand hearts—the fond, deep love of one—
The hopes that dance around a life whose charms are but begun--
They lighted up her chestnut eye, they mantle o'er her cheek,
They sparkle on her open brow, and high soul'd joy bespeak.

Ah! who shall blame, if scarce that day, through all its brilliant
   hours,
She thought of that quiet convent's calm, its sunshine and its flowers?

PART II.

It was a labouring bark that slowly held its way,
And o'er its lee the coast of France in the light of evening lay;
And on its deck a lady sat, who gazed with tearful eyes
Upon the fast-receding hills, that dim and distant rise.
No marvel that the lady wept—there was no land on earth
She loved like that dear land, although she owed it not her birth;
It was her mother's land, the land of childhood and of friends—
It was the land where she had found for all her griefs amends—
The land where her dead husband slept—the land where she had
   known
The tranquil convent's hush'd repose, and the splendours of a throne:
No marvel that the lady wept—it was the land of France—
The chosen home of chivalry—the garden of romance!
The past was bright, like those dear hills so far behind her bark;
The future, like the gathering night, was ominous and dark!
One gaze again—one long, last gaze—"Adieu, fair France, to
   thee!"
The breeze comes forth—she is alone on the unconscious sea.

The scene was changed.   It was an eve of raw and surly mood,
And in a turret-chamber high of ancient Holyrood
Sat Mary, listening to the rain, and sighing with the winds,
That seem'd to suit the stormy state of men's uncertain minds.
The touch of care that blanch'd her cheek—her smile was sadder
   now,
The weight of royalty had press'd too heavy on her brow;
And traitors to her councils came, and rebels to the field;
The Stuart *sceptre* well she sway'd, but the *sword* she could not
   wield.
She thought of all her blighted hopes—the dreams of youth's brief
   day,
And summon'd Rizzio with his lute, and bade the minstrel play

The songs she lov'd in early years—the songs of gay Navarre,
The songs perchance that erst were sung by gallant Chatelar:
They half beguiled her of her cares, they soothed her into smiles,
They won her thoughts from bigot zeal, and fierce domestic broils:—
But hark! the tramp of armed men! the Douglas battle-cry!
They come—they come—and lo! the scowl of Ruthven's hollow eye!
And swords are drawn, and daggers gleam, and tears and words are
    vain,
The ruffian steel is in his heart—the faithful Rizzio's slain!
Then Mary Stuart brush'd aside the tears that trickling fell!
"Now for my father's arm!" she said; "my woman's heart fare-
well!"

The scene was changed. It was a lake, with one small lonely isle,
And there within the prison-walls of its baronial pile,
Stern men stood menacing their queen, till she should stoop to sign
The traitorous scroll that snatch'd the crown from her ancestral
    line:—
"My lords, my lords!" the captive said, "were I but once more free,
With ten good knights on yonder shore, to aid my cause and me,
That parchment would I scatter wide to every breeze that blows,
And once more reign a Stuart queen o'er my remorseless foes!"
A red spot burn'd upon her cheek—stream'd her rich tresses down,
She wrote the words—she stood erect—a queen without a crown!

PART III.

The scene was changed. A royal host a royal banner bore,
And the faithful of the land stood round their smiling queen once
    more.
She staid her steed upon a hill—she saw them marching by—
She heard their shouts—she read success in every flashing eye;—
The tumult of the strife begins—it roars—it dies away;
And Mary's troops, and banners now, and courtiers—where are they?
Scatter'd and strewn, and flying far defenceless and undone—
O God! to see what she has lost, and think what guilt has won!
Away! away! thy gallant steed must act no laggard's part;
Yet vain his speed, for thou dost bear the arrow in thy heart.

The scene was changed.   Beside the block a sullen headsman stood,
And gleam'd the broad axe in his hand, that soon must drip with
   blood.
With slow and steady step there came a lady through the hall,
And breathless silence chain'd the lips, and touch'd the hearts of all:
Rich were the sable robes she wore—her white veil round her fell—
And from her neck there hung a cross—the cross she loved so well !
I knew that queenly form again, though blighted was its bloom—
I saw that grief had deck'd it out—an offering for the tomb !
I knew the eye, though faint its light, that once so brightly shone—
I knew the voice, though feeble now, that thrill'd with every tone—
I knew the ringlets, almost grey, once threads of living gold—
I knew that bounding grace of step—that symmetry of mould !
Even now I see her far away, in that calm convent aisle,
I hear her chant her vesper-hymn, I mark her holy smile—
Even now I see her bursting forth, upon her bridal morn,
A new star in the firmament, to light and glory born !
Alas! the change! she placed her foot upon a triple throne,
And on the scaffold now she stands—beside the block, *alone!*
The little dog that licks her hand, the last of all the crowd
Who sunn'd themselves beneath her glance, and round her footsteps
   bow'd !
Her neck is bared—the blow is struck—the soul is pass'd away;
The bright—the beautiful—is now a bleeding piece of clay !
The dog is moaning piteously; and, as it gurgles o'er,
Laps the warm blood that trickling runs unheeded to the floor !
The blood of beauty, wealth, and power—the heart-blood of a
   queen—
The noblest of the Stuart race—the fairest earth had seen—
Lapp'd by a dog !   Go, think of it, in silence and alone;
Then weigh against a grain of sand the glories of a throne!

A SCOTTISH TEA-PARTY.

By J. D. Carrick

Now let's sing how Miss M'Wharty,
T'other evening had a party,
  To have a cup of tea;
And how she had collected
All the friends that she respected,
  All as merry as merry could be.
Dames and damsels came in dozens,
With two-three country cousins,
  In their lily-whites so gay;
Just to sit and chitter-chatter,
O'er a cup of scalding water,
  In the fashion of the day.

(*Spoken in different female voices.*)   "Dear me, how ha'e ye been this lang time, mem?"   "Pretty weel, I thank ye, mem. How ha'e ye been yoursel?"   "Oh, mem, I've been vera ill wi' the rheumatisms, and though I were your tippet, I couldna be fu'er o' *stitches* than I am; but whan did ye see Mrs. Pinkerton?" "Oh, mem, I ha'ena seen her this lang time. Did ye no hear that Mrs. Pinkerton and I ha'e had a difference?"   "No, mem, I didna hear. What was't about, mem?"   "I'll tell you what it was about, mem. I gaed o'er to ca' upon her ae day, and when I gaed in, ye see, she's sitting feeding the parrot, and I says to her, 'Mrs. Pinkerton, how d'ye do, mem?' and she never let on she heard me; and I says again, 'Mrs. Pinkerton, how d'ye do?' I says; and wi' that she turns about, and says she, 'Mrs. M'Saunter, I'm really astonished you should come and ask me how I do, considering the manner you've ridiculed me and my husband in public companies!'   'Mrs. Pinkerton,' quo' I, 'what's that ye mean, mem?' and then she began and gied me a' the ill-mannered abuse you can possibly conceive.   And I just says to her, quo' I, 'Mrs. Pinkerton,' quo' I, 'that's no what I cam' to hear; and if that's the way ye intend to gae on,' quo' I, 'I wish ye gude morning;' so I

comes awa'. Now I'll tell ye what a' this was about. Ye see, it
was just about the term time, ye ken, they flitted aboon us, and I
gaed up on the term morning to see if they wanted a kettle boiled
or anything o' that kind; and when I gaed in, Mr. Pinkerton, he's
sitting in the middle o' the floor, and the barber's shaving him,
and the barber had laid a' his face round wi' the *white* saip; and
Mr. Pinkerton, ye ken, has a very *red* nose, and the red nose
sticking through the white saip, just put me in mind o' a *carrot*
sticking through a *collyflower;* and I very innocently happened to
mention this in a party where I had been dining, and some officious
body's gane and tell't Mrs. Pinkerton, and Mrs. Pinkerton's ta'en
this *wonderfully* amiss. What d'ye think o' Mrs. Pinks?'" "Deed,
mem, she's no worth your while; but did you hear what happened
to Mrs. Clapperton the ither day?" "No mem, what's happened
to her, poor body?" "I'll tell you that, mem. You see, she
was coming down Montrose Street, and she had on a red pelisse and
a white muff; and there's a bubbly-jock* coming out o' the breweree
—and whether the red pelisse had ta'en the beast's eye or no, I
dinna ken, but the bubbly-jock rins after Mrs. Clapperton, and
Mrs. Clapperton ran, poor body, and the bubbly-jock after her,
and in crossing the causey, ye see, her fit slippet, and the muff
flew frae her, and there's a cart coming past, and the wheel o' the
cart gaes o'er the muff; and ae gentleman rins and lifts Mrs. Clapperton, and anither lifts the muff; and when he looks into the muff,
what's there, but a wee bit broken bottle, wi' a wee soup brandy
in 't; and the gentlemen fell a looking and laughing to ane anither,
and they're gaun about to their dinner parties and their supper
parties, and telling about Mrs. Clapperton wi' the bubbly-jock and
the bottle o' brandy. Now it's vera ill done o' the gentlemen to
do anything o' the kind; for Mrs. Clapperton was just like to drap
down wi' perfect vexation; for she's a body o' that kind o'
laithfu' kind o' disposition, she would just as soon take aquafortis
as she would take brandy in ony clandestine kind o' manner."

> Each gemman at his post now,
> In handing tea or toast now,
> Is striving to outshine;

* Turkey-cock.

While keen to find a handle
To tip a little scandal,
     The ladies all combine—
Of this one's dress or carriage,
Or t'other's death or marriage,
     The dear chit chat's kept up;
While the lady from the table
Is calling while she's able—
     " Will you have another cup?"

" Dear me, you're no done, mem—you'll take another cup, mem—take out your spoon." " Oh no, mem, I never take mair than ae cup upon ony occasion." " Toots, sic nonsense." " You may toots awa, but it's true sense, mem. And whan did ye see Mrs. Petticraw, mem?" " 'Deed, I ha'ena seen her this lang time, and I'm no wanting to see her; she's a body o' that kind, that just gangs frae house to house gathering clashes, and gets her tea here and her tea there, and tells in your house what she hears in mine, and when she begins, she claver clavers on and on, and the claver just comes frae her as if it cam' aff a *clew*, and there's nae end o' her." " Oh, you maun excuse her, poor body—ye ken she's lost a' her *teeth*, and her tongue *wearies* in her mouth wantin' *company*." " 'Deed, they may excuse her that wants her, for it's no me. Oh ! ladies, did ye hear what's happened in Mr. M'Farlane's family ? There's an awfu' circumstance happened in that family,—Mr. and Mrs. M'Farlane havena spoken to ane anither for this fortnight, and I'll tell you the reason o't. Mrs. M'Farlane, poor body, had lost ane o' her teeth, and she gaed awa to the dentist to get a tooth put in, and the dentist showed her twa or three kinds o' them, and amang the rest he showed her a Waterloo ane ; and she thought she would ha'e a Waterloo ane, poor body. Weel, the dentist puts in ane to her, and the tooth's running in her head a' day, and when she gangs to her bed at nicht, as she tells me—but I'm certain she must have been dreaming—just about ane or twa o'clock o' the morning, mem, just about ane or twa o'clock in the morning, when she looks out o' her bed, there's a *great lang* sodger standing at the bedside; and quo' she, ' Man, what are ye wanting?' she says. Quo' he, ' Mrs. M'Farlane, that's my

tooth that ye've got in your mouth.' 'Your tooth!' quo' she, 'the
very tooth that I bought the day at the dentist's!' 'It doesna
matter for that,' quo' he, 'I lost it at Waterloo.' 'Ye lost it at
Waterloo, sic nonsense!' Weel, wi' that he comes forret to pit
his finger into Mrs. M'Farlane's mouth to tak' the tooth out o' her
mouth, and she gies a snap, and catch'd him by the finger, and he
gied a great screich and took her a gowf i' the side o' the head,
and that waukened her; and when she waukens, what has she
gotten but Mr. M'Farlane's finger atween her teeth, and him roaring
like to gang out o' his judgment! Noo, Mr. M'Farlane has been
gaun about wi' his thumb in a clout, and looking as surly as a
bear; for he thinks Mrs. M'Farlane had done it out o' spite, because
he wadna let her buy a sofa at a sale the other day; noo, it's
vera ill-done o' Mr. M'Farlane to think ony thing o' that kind, as
if ony woman would gang and *bite* her ain *flesh* and *blood* if she
kent o't."

> Miss M'Wharty, with a smile,
> Asks the ladies to beguile
>   An hour with whist or loo;
> While old uncle cries, " Don't plague us;
> Bring the toddy and the negus—
>   We'll have a song or two."
> " Oh dear me, uncle Joseph!
> Pray do not snap one's nose off;
>   You'll have toddy when your dry,
> With a little ham and chicken,
> An' some other dainty pickin'
>   For the ladies, by-and-by."

" Weel, mem, how's your frien' Mrs. Howdyson coming on in
thae times, when there is sae muckle influenza gaun about amang
families?" "Mrs. Howdyson! na, ye maun ask somebody that kens
better about her than I do. I ha'e na seen Mrs. Howdyson for three
months." "Dear me! do ye tell me sae? you that used to be like
twa sisters! How did sic a wonderfu' change as that come about?"
"'Deed, mem, it was a very silly matter did it a'. Some five
months since, ye see, mem (but ye maunna be speaking about it),

Mrs. Howdyson called on me ae forenoon, and after sitting awhile she drew a paper parcel out o' her muff:—'Ye'll no ken what this is?' said she. 'No,' quo' I, 'it's no very likely.' 'Weel, it's my worthy husband's satin breeks, that he had on the day we were married; and I'm gaun awa' to Miss Gushat to get her to mak' them into a bonnet for mysel', for I ha'e a great respect for them on account of him that's awa'.' Respect! thinks I to mysel (for about this time she was spoke o' wi' Deacon Purdie), queer kind o' respect! —trying to catch a new gudeman wi' a bonnet made out o' the auld ane's breeks!—but I said naething. Weel, twa or three weeks after this, I was taking a walk wi' anither lady, and wha should we meet but Mrs. Howdyson, wi' a fine, flashy black satin bonnet on! So, we stopped, and chatted about the weather, and the great mortality that was in the town; and when shaking hands wi' her at parting, I, without meaning ony ill, ga'e a nod at her bonnet, and happened to say, in my thoughtless kind o' way, 'Is that the breeks?' never mindin' at the time that there was a stranger lady wi' me. Now, this was maybe wrang in me; but, considering our intimacy, I never dreamed she had ta'en't amiss—till twa three Sundays after, I met her gaun to the kirk alang wi' Miss Purdie, and I happened to ha'e on ane o' the new fashionable bonnets—really, it was an elegantly-shaped bonnet! and trimmed in the most tasteful and becoming manner—it was, in short, such a bonnet as ony lady might have been proud to be seen in. Weel, for a' that, mem, we hadna stood lang before she began on my poor bonnet, and called it a' the ugly-looking things she could think o', and advised me to gang hame and change it, for I looked sae vulgar and daft-like in't. At length, I got nettled at her abuse, for I kent it was a' out o' spite. 'Mrs. Howdyson,' says I, 'the bonnet may be baith vulgar and daft-like, as you say, but I'm no half sae vulgar or sae daft-like as I wad be if, like *some folks*, I were gaun to the kirk wi' a *pair o' auld breeks on my head!*' So, I turns on my heel and left them; but though it was the Sabbath-day, I could not help thinking to mysel—my lady, I trow I've gi'en you a lozenge to sook that'll keep you frae sleeping, better than ony confectionary you've ta'en to the kirk wi' ye this while."

"Weel, ladies, there are some strange kind o' folks to be met with after a'. I've just been listening to your crack, and it puts me in mind of a new-married lady I was visiting the ither day. Before she was married, she was one of the dressiest belles we had about the town; and as for changing bonnets, you would seldom meet her twice wi' the same ane on. But now, though she has been little mair than three months married, she has become one of the most idle tawpie drabs that ever was seen, and has so many romantic fancies and stupid conceits about her, that I often canna help pitying the poor husband. Besides, she kens nae mair about house matters than if she had never heard o' sic things. She was an only dochter, you see, and, like the ewe's pet lamb, she got mair *licking* than *learning*. Just to gie ye an instance o' her management,—she told me she was making preparations for a dinner that her husband was going to give in a day or twa; and amang other things, she said that he wanted a turkey in ruffles. 'Turkey in ruffles!' quo' I, 'that's a queer kind o' a dish.' 'Queer as it is, I'll manage it.' 'I would like to see it,' quo' I. So wi' that, she rings the bell and orders the servant to bring it ben. Weel, what's this but a turkey; the feathers were aff, to be sure, which showed some sma' glimmering o' sense, but the neck o' the beast was a' done up wi' fine cambric ruffles; these were to be ta'en aff, it seems, till it was roasted, and then it was to get on a' its finery again, so as to appear in full puff before the company; and this was what she called a turkey in ruffles! 'Dear me!' quo' I, 'this is a way o' *dressing* a turkey I never saw before—I'm thinking the gudeman must have meant turkey and truffles.'—'Truffles!' cried she, looking like a bewildered goose, 'and what's truffles, in a' the world?' 'Just look your cookery-book,' quo' I, 'and you'll find that truffles are not made o' cambric muslin.' Now, ladies, did you ever hear such ignorance? but, better than that, she went on to tell me how she had sent the servant to the market to buy a hare, to mak' soup o'; but, says she, 'What do you think the stupid creature did? instead of a hare, she brought me twa rabbits; now, ye ken, mem, rabbits dinna mak' gude hare-soup.' 'No,' quo' I; '*hare-soup* made o' *rabbits* may be a rare dish, but it's no to my taste.' 'That's just my opinion; so, as they're gey and white in the flesh, I'm thinking just to make a bit veal-pie o' them; —what do you think o' that for economy?' 'Excellent,' quo' I, 'if you can *manage* it.' 'But,' said she, 'I'm to ha'e a haggis too, as a novelty to some English gentlemen that are to be of the party; now, I'm thinking of having the bag of the haggis dyed turkey-red; it's a fancy o' my ain, and I think it would astonish them; besides, it would cut such a dash on the table.' 'Dash on the table!' quo' I, 'nae doubt it would cut a dash on the table;—but wha ever heard o' a turkey-red haggis before?' Now, I think, ladies, if my frien' can either make *hare-soup* or a *veal-pie* out of a pair of *rabbits*, she'll be even a greater genius than Mrs. Howdyson, wi' her new bonnet made out o' a pair of auld breeks!"

> So thus to sit and chitter chatter
> O'er a cup o' scalding water,
> Is the fashion o' the day.

From " Whistle Binkie," by permission of the Publisher.

TAM O' SHANTER.

By Robert Burns.

When chapmen billies leave the street,
And drouthy neebors neebors meet,
As market-days are wearin' late,
An' folk begin to tak' the gate;
While we sit bousing at the nappy,
An' getting fou' and unco happy,
We think na on the lang Scots miles,
The mosses, waters, slaps, an' stiles
That lie between us and our hame,
Whare sits our sulky, sullen dame,
Gathering her brows like gathering storm,
Nursing her wrath to keep it warm.

This truth fand honest Tam o' Shanter,
As he frae Ayr ae night did canter,
(Auld Ayr, wham ne'er a town surpasses
For honest men and bonnie lasses).

O Tam, hadst thou but been sae wise
As ta'en thy ain wife Kate's advice!
She tauld thee weel thou was a skellum,
A blethering, blustering, drunken blellum;
That frae November to October,
Ae market-day thou was nae sober;
That ilka melder wi' the miller,
Thou sat as lang as thou had siller;
That every naig was ca'd a shoe on,
The smith and thee gat roaring fou' on;
That at the Lord's house, e'en on Sunday,
Thou drank wi' Kirkton Jean till Monday.
She prophesied that, late or soon,
Thou wad be found deep drown'd in Doon;
Or catch'd wi' warlocks in the mirk,
By Alloway's auld haunted kirk.

Ah, gentle dames, it gars me greet,
To think how mony counsels sweet,
How mony lengthen'd sage advices
The husband frae the wife despises!

But to our tale.   Ae market night,
Tam had got planted unco right
Fast by an ingle bleezing finely,
Wi' reaming swats, that drank divinely;
And at his elbow Souter Johnny,
His ancient, trusty, drouthy crony:
Tam lo'ed him like a vera brither;
They had been fou' for weeks thegither.
The night drave on wi' sangs and clatter,
And aye the ale was growing better;
The landlady and Tam grew gracious,
Wi' favours secret, sweet, and precious;
The Souter tauld his queerest stories;
The landlord's laugh was ready chorus;
The storm without might rair and rustle,
Tam didna mind the storm a whistle.

Care, mad to see a man sae happy,
E'en drown'd himself amang the nappy.
As bees flee hame wi' lades o' treasure,
The minutes wing'd their way wi' pleasure.
Kings may be blest, but Tam was glorious,
O'er a' the ills o' life victorious.

But pleasures are like poppies spread—
You seize the flower, its bloom is shed;
Or like the snow-fall in the river—
A moment white, then melts for ever;
Or like the borealis race,
That flit ere you can point their place;
Or like the rainbow's lovely form,
Evanishing amid the storm.

Nae man can tether time nor tide:
The hour approaches Tam maun ride;
That hour, o' night's black arch the keystane,
That dreary hour he mounts his beast in;
And sic a night he taks the road in,
As ne'er poor sinner was abroad in.
The wind blew as 'twad blawn its last;
The rattling showers rose on the blast;
The speedy gleams the darkness swallow'd;
Loud, deep, and lang the thunder bellow'd:
That night a child might understand
The deil had business on his hand.

Weel mounted on his grey mare, Meg
(A better never lifted leg),
Tam skelpit on through dub and mire,
Despising wind, and rain, and fire;
Whiles hauding fast his gude blue bonnet,
Whiles crooning o'er some auld Scots sonnet;
Whiles glow'ring round wi' prudent care,
Lest bogles catch him unaware:
Kirk-Alloway was drawing nigh,
Whare ghaists and houlets nightly cry.

D

By this time he was 'cross the ford,
Whare, in the snaw, the chapman smoor'd;
And past the birks and meikle stane,
Whare drucken Charlie brak 's neck-bane;
And through the whins, and by the cairn,
Whare hunters fand the murder'd bairn;
And near the thorn aboon the well,
Whare Mungo's mither hang'd hersel'.——
Before him Doon pours all his floods;
The doubling storm roars through the woods;
The lightnings flash from pole to pole;
Near and more near the thunders roll;
When, glimmering thro' the groaning trees,
Kirk-Alloway seem'd in a bleeze;
Through ilka bore the beams were glancing,
And loud resounded mirth and dancing.

Inspiring bold John Barleycorn!
What dangers thou canst make us scorn!
Wi' tippeny we fear nae evil;
Wi' usquebae we 'll face the devil.
The swats sae ream'd in Tammie's noddle,
Fair play, he cared nae deils a bodle;
But Maggie stood right sair astonish'd,
Till, by the heel and hand admonish'd,
She ventured forward on the light,
And, wow, Tam saw an' unco sight!
Warlocks and witches in a dance!
Nae cotillon brent-new frae France,
But hornpipes, jigs, strathspeys and reels
Put life and mettle in their heels.
A winnock-bunker in the east,
There sat auld Nick in shape o' beast;
A towzie tyke, black, grim, an large,
To gie them music was his charge:
He screw'd his pipes, and gart them skirl,
Till roof an' rafters a' did dirl.

Coffins stood round like open presses,
That shaw'd the dead in their last dresses;
And by some devilish cantrip sleight,
Each in his cauld hand held a light,
By which heroic Tam was able
To note upon the haly table,
A murderer's banes in gibbet-airns;
Twa span-lang, wee unchristen'd bairns;
A thief, new-cutted frae a rape,
Wi' his last gasp his gab did gape;
Five tomahawks, wi' blude red-rusted;
Five scimitars, wi' murder crusted;
A garter, which a babe had strangled;
A knife a father's throat had mangled,
Whom his ain son o' life bereft,
The grey hairs yet stak to the heft;
Wi' mair o' horrible and awfu',
Which ev'n to name wad be unlawfu'.

As Tammie glow'r'd, amazed and curious,
The mirth and fun grew fast and furious;
The piper loud and louder blew;
The dancers quick and quicker flew;
They reel'd, they set, they cross'd, they cleekit,
Till ilka carlin swat and reekit,
And coost her duddies to the wark,
And linkit at it in her sark!

Now, Tam, O Tam! had thae been queans,
A' plump and strappin', in their teens;
Their sarks, instead o' creeshie flannen,
Been snaw-white se'enteen-hunder linen,
Thir breeks o' mine, my only pair,
That ance were plush, o' gude blue hair,
I wad ha'e gi'en them aff my hurdies
For ae blink o' the bonnie burdies!

But wither'd beldams, auld and droll
Rigwoodie hags wad spean a foal,

Louping and flinging on a cummock,
I wonder didna turn thy stomach.

But Tam kenn'd what was what fu' brawlie.
There was ae winsome wench and walie
That night enlisted in the core
(Lang after kenn'd on Carrick shore;
For mony a beast to dead she shot,
And perish'd mony a bonnie boat,
And shook baith muckle corn and bear,
And kept the country side in fear);
Her cutty-sark, o' Paisley harn,
That while a lassie she had worn,
In longitude tho' sorely scanty,
It was her best, and she was vauntie—
Ah! little kenn'd thy reverend grannie,
That sark she coft for her wee Nannie,
Wi' twa pund Scots ('twas a' her riches),
Wad ever grace a dance o' witches!

But here my Muse her wing maun cow'r;
Sic flights are far beyond her power;
To sing how Nannie lap and flang,
(A supple jade she was and strang),
And how Tam stood like ane bewitch'd,
And thought his very een enrich'd;
Even Satan glow'r'd and fidg'd fu' fain,
And hotch'd and blew wi' might and main,
Till first ae caper, syne anither,
Tam tint his reason a' thegither,
And roars out, " Weel done, Cutty-sark!"
And in an instant a' was dark:
And scarcely had he Maggie rallied,
When out the hellish legion sallied.

As bees bizz out wi' angry fyke,
When plundering herds assail their byke;
As open pussie's mortal foes,
When, pop! she starts before their nose;

As eager runs the market-crowd,
When " Catch the thief !" resounds aloud;
So Maggie runs, the witches follow,
Wi' mony an eldritch screech and hollow.

Ah, Tam! ah, Tam! thou'lt get thy fairin';
In hell they'll roast thee like a herrin'!
In vain thy Kate awaits thy comin'!
Kate soon will be a waefu' woman!
Now, do thy speedy utmost, Meg,
And win the key-stane o' the brig;
There at them thou thy tail may toss,
A running stream they darena cross:
But ere the key-stane she could make,
The fient a tail she had to shake!
For Nannie, far before the rest,
Hard upon noble Maggie prest,
And flew at Tam with furious ettle,
But little wist she Maggie's mettle—
Ae spring brought off her master hale,
But left behind her ain grey tail:
The carlin claught her by the rump,
And left poor Maggie scarce a stump.

Now, wha this tale o' truth shall read,
Ilk man and mother's son, take heed:
Whene'er to drink ye are inclin'd,
Or cutty-sarks run in your mind,
Think, ye maun buy the joys owre dear,
Remember Tam o' Shanter's mare.

THE ELDER'S DEATH-BED.

By Professor Wilson.

FOR six years' Sabbaths I had seen the elder in his
accustomed place beneath the pulpit; and, with a sort of

solemn fear, had looked on his steadfast countenance, during sermon, psalm, and prayer. I met the pastor going to pray by his death-bed; and, with the privilege which nature gives us to behold, even in their last extremity, the loving and beloved, I turned to accompany him to the house of sorrow, of resignation, and of death.

And now, for the first time, I observed, walking close to the feet of his horse, a little boy about ten years of age, who kept frequently looking up in the pastor's face, with his blue eyes bathed in tears. A changeful expression of grief, hope, and despair, made almost pale, cheeks which otherwise were blooming in health and beauty; and I recognized, in the small features and smooth forehead of childhood, a resemblance to the aged man, who, we understood, was now lying on his death-bed. "They had to send his grandson for me through the snow, mere child as he is," said the minister, looking tenderly on the boy; "but love makes the young heart bold;—and there is ONE who tempers the wind to the shorn lamb."

As we slowly approached the cottage through a deep snow-drift, we saw, peeping out from the door, brothers and sisters of our little guide, who quickly disappeared; and then their mother showed herself in their stead, expressing, by her raised eyes and arms folded across her breast, how thankful she was to see, at last, the pastor,—beloved in joy and trusted in trouble.

A few words sufficed to say who was the stranger; and the dying man, blessing me by name, held out to me his cold shrivelled hand, in token of recognition. I took my seat at a small distance from the bedside, and left a closer station for those who were more dear. The pastor

sat down near his elder's head; and by the bed, leaning
on it with gentle hands, stood that matron, his daughter-
in-law—a figure that would have sainted a higher dwelling,
and whose native beauty was now more touching in its
grief.

"If the storm do not abate," said the sick man, after a
pause, "it will be hard for my friends to carry me over
the drifts to the church-yard." This sudden approach to
the grave struck, as with a bar of ice, the heart of the
loving boy; and, with a long deep sigh, he fell down, his
face like ashes, on the bed; while the old man's palsied
right hand had just strength enough to lay itself upon his
head. "God has been gracious to me a sinner!" said
the dying man. "During thirty years that I have been
an elder in your church, never have I missed sitting there
one Sabbath. When the mother of my children was
taken from me, it was on a Tuesday she died, and on
Saturday she was buried. We stood together, when my
Alice was let down into the narrow house made for all
living. On the Sabbath I joined in the public worship
of God. She commanded me to do so, the night before
she went away. I could not join in the psalm that
Sabbath, for her voice was not in the throng. Her grave
was covered up, and grass and flowers grew there."

The old man then addressed himself to his grandchild:
—"Jamie, thy own father has forgotten thee in thy
infancy, and me in my old age; but, Jamie, forget not
thou thy father or thy mother; for that, thou knowest
and feelest, is the commandment of God."

The broken-hearted boy could give no reply. He
had gradually stolen closer and closer unto the loving
old man; and was now lying, worn out with sorrow,

drenched and dissolved in tears, in his grandfather's bosom. His mother sunk down on her knees, and hid her face with her hand. " Oh! if my husband knew but of this, he would never, never desert his dying father!" And I now knew that the elder was praying, on his death-bed, for a disobedient and wicked son.

The door was suddenly opened, and a tall fine-looking man entered; but with a lowering and dark countenance, seemingly in sorrow, in misery, and remorse. Agitated, confounded, and awe-struck by the melancholy scene, he sat down on a chair, and looked with a ghastly face towards his father's death-bed. The elder said with a solemn voice, " Thou art come in time to receive thy father's blessing. May the remembrance of what will happen in this room, before the morning again shine over the Hazel-glen, win thee from the error of thy ways! Thou art here to witness the mercy of thy God and thy Saviour, WHOM THOU HAST FORGOTTEN."

The young man with much effort advanced to the bedside; and at last found voice to say, " Father, I am not without the affections of nature; and I hurried home the moment I heard that the minister had been seen riding towards our house. I hope that you will yet recover; and if I have ever made you unhappy, I ask your forgiveness; for, though I may not think as you do on matters of religion, I have a human heart. Father, I may have been unkind, but I am not cruel. I ask your forgiveness."

" Come near to me, William; kneel down by the bed-side, and let my hand feel the head of my beloved son; for blindness is coming fast upon me. Thou wast my first-born, and thou art my only living child. All thy brothers and sisters are lying in the church-yard beside her whose sweet face thine own, William, did once so much resemble. Long wast thou the joy, the pride of my soul,—ay, too much the pride; for there was not in all the parish such a man, such a son, as my own William. If thy heart has since changed, God may inspire it again with right thoughts. I have sorely wept for thee—ay, William, when there was none near me;—even as David wept for Absalom—for thee, my son! my son!"

A long deep groan was the only reply; but the whole body of the kneeling man was convulsed; and it was easy to see his sufferings, his contrition, his remorse, and his despair. The pastor said, with a sterner voice and austerer countenance than were natural to him,—" Know you whose hand is now lying on your rebellious head? But what signifies the word 'father' to him who has denied God, the Father of us all?" " Oh! press him not too hardly," said his weeping wife, coming forward from a dark corner of the room, where she tried to conceal herself in grief, fear, and shame. " Spare, oh! spare my husband!—he has ever been kind to ME;" and with that she knelt down beside him, with her long, soft, white arms, mournfully and affectionately laid across his neck. " Go thou likewise, my sweet little Jamie," said the elder, " go even out of my bosom, and kneel down beside thy father and thy mother; so that I may bless you all at once, and with one yearning prayer." The child did as the solemn voice commanded, and knelt down somewhat timidly by his father's side; nor did the unhappy man decline encircling with his arm his son, too much neglected, but still dear to him as his own blood—in spite of the deadening and debasing influence of infidelity!

"Put the Word of God into the hands of my son, and let him read aloud, to his dying father, the eleventh chapter of the Gospel according to St. John." The pastor went up to the kneelers, and said,—"There was a time when none, William, could read the Scriptures better than couldst thou;—can it be that the son of my friend hath forgotten the lessons of his youth?" He had not forgotten them; there was no need of the repentant sinner to lift up his eyes from the bedside. The sacred stream of the Gospel had worn a channel in his heart, and the waters were again flowing. With a choked voice, he read,—"Jesus said unto her, I am the resurrection and the life; and whosoever liveth, and believeth in me, shall never die. Believest thou this? She said unto him, Yea, Lord: I believe thou art the Christ, the Son of God, which should come into the world."

"That is not an unbeliever's voice," said the dying man, triumphantly; "nor, William, hast thou an unbeliever's heart. Say that thou believest in what thou hast read, and thy father will die happy!" "I do believe, and as THOU forgivest me, so may I be forgiven by my FATHER who is in heaven." The elder seemed like a man suddenly inspired with a new life. His faded eyes kindled,—his pale cheeks glowed,—his palsied hands seemed to wax strong,—and his voice was clear as that of manhood in its prime. "Into Thy hands, O God! I commit my spirit—" and so·saying, he gently sank back on his pillow; and I thought I heard a sigh. There was then a long, deep silence; and the father, the mother, and the child, rose from their knees. The eyes of us all were turned towards the white, placid face of the figure, now **stretched in everlasting rest; and without lamentations,** save the silent lamentations of the resigned soul, we stood around THE DEATH-BED OF THE ELDER.

JEAN FINLATER'S LOUN.

By William Anderson.

THE winter was lang, an' the seed time was late,
An' the cauld month o' March sealed Tam Finlater's fate;
He dwin'd like a sna' wreath till some time in June,
Then left Jean a widow, wi' ae raggit loun.
Jean scrapit a livin' wi' weavin' at shanks—
Jock got into scrapes—he was aye playin' pranks;
Frae the Dee to the Don he was fear'd roun' the toun—
A reckless young scamp was Jean Finlater's loun.

Jock grew like a saugh on a saft, boggy brae—
He dislikit the school, and car'd mair for his play;
Ony mischief that happened, abroad or at hame,
Whaever was guilty, Jock aye got the blame.
Gin a lantern or lozen was crackit or broke,
Nae ane i' the toun got the wite o't, but Jock;
If a dog was to hang, or a kitlin to droon,
They wad cry, "Gie the job to Jean Finlater's loun."

He rappit the knockers—he rang a' the bells—
Sent dogs doun the causeway wi' pans at their tails:
The dykes o' the gardens an' orchards he scaled—
The apples, an' berries, and cherries he stealed.
Gin a claise rope was cuttit, or pole ta'en awa,
The neighbours declared it was Jock did it a';
Wi' his thum' at his nose, street or lane he ran doun—
A rigwoodie deil was Jean Finlater's loun.

He pelted the peatmen, e'en wi' their ain peats—
Pu'd hair frae their horse tails, then laughed at their threats;

An' on Christmas-nicht, frae the Shiprow to Shore,
He claikit wi' sowens ilka shutter and door.
We ha'e chairs in our college for law and theology;
If ane had been vacant for trick or prankology,
Without a dissent ye 'd hae votit the goun,
To sic an adept as Jean Finlater's loun.

On the forenoons o' Fridays he aften was seen
Coupin' country fowks carts upside doun i' the Green
An', where masons were workin', without ony fear,
He shoudit wi' scaffoldin' planks ower their meer.
To harrie birds' nests he wad travel for miles,
Ding owre dykes an' hedges, an' brak doun the stiles,
Swing on gentlemen's yetts, or their pailin's pu' doun;
Tricks and mischief were meat to Jean Finlater's loun.

He vext Betty Osley, wha threatened the law—
Ritchie Marchant wad chase him an' had him in awe;
Frae the Hardgate to Fittie he aye was in scrapes
An' a' body wondered how Jock made escapes.
Jean said he was royet, *that* she maun aloo,
But he wad grow wiser the aulder he grew;
She aye took his part against a' body roun',
For she kent that her Jock was a kind-hearted loun.

At seventeen, Jock was a stout, strappin' chiel,
He had left aff his pranks, an' was now doin' weel;
In his face there was health, in his arm there was pith,
An' he learned to be baith a farrier an' smith.
His character, noo, was unstained wi' a blot,
His early delinquencies a' were forgot,
Till the weel-keepit birthday of Geordie cam' roun',
Which markit the fate o' Jean Finlater's loun.

The fire-warks were ower, an' the bonfire brunt done,
An' the crowd to Meg Dickie's gaed seekin' mair fun;
They attackit the White Ship, in rear an' in front—
Took tables and chairs, whilk they broke an' they brunt.

Jock couldna resist it—he brunt an' he broke—
Some sax were made prisoners—amang them was Jock;
Ten days in the jail, an' his miseries to croun,
Bread an' water was fare for Jean Finlater's loun.

Jock entered the Life-Guards—bade Scotland adieu—
Fought bravely for laurels at fam'd Waterloo;
An' his conduct was such that, e'er five years had past,
He was made, by Lord II——, master-farrier at last.
Jean's rent aye was paid; an' she still was alive
To see her brave son in the year twenty-five;
An' nane wad ha'e kent that the whisker'd dragoon
Was the same tricky nickem—Jean Finlater's loun.

Copyright.

THE TWENTY-THIRD PSALM.

TRANSLATED FROM HEBREW INTO SCOTTISH, BY THE REV.
P. HATELY WADDELL, LL.D.

1 The LORD *is* my herd, nae want sal fa' me:

2 He louts me till lie amang green howes; he airts me atowre by the lown watirs:

3 He waukens my wa'-gaen saul; he weises me roun, for his ain name's sake, intil right roddins.

4 Na! tho' I gang thro' the dead-mirk-dail; *e'en thar* sal I dread nae skaithin: for yersel *are* nar-by me; yer stok an' yer stay haud me baith fu' cheerie.

5 My buird ye ha'e hansell'd in face o' my faes; ye ha'e drookit my head wi' oyle; my bicker is *fu' an'* skailin'.

6 E'en sae, sal gude-guidin' an' gude-gree gang wi' me, ilk day o' my livin'; an' evir mair syne, i' the LORD's ain howff, *at lang last,* sal I mak' bydan.—*By permission, from "Psalms frae Hebrew intil Scottis."*

THE ANNUITY.

By George Outram.

"The little work from which the 'Annuity' has been selected was printed for private distribution only, by the late Mr. George Outram. It bears the unpromising title of *Legal Lyrics, and Metrical Illustrations of the Scottish Forms of Process;* but abounds in keen wit and rich humour, which force themselves on the appreciation even of readers whose misfortune it is to be born south of the Tweed, and to be unacquainted with the exquisitely simple forms and phrases of Scottish law."—*Wills.*

I GAED to spend a week in Fife—
   An unco week it proved to be—
For there I met a waesome wife
   Lamentin' her viduity.
Her grief brak out sae fierce and fell,
I thought her heart wad burst the shell;
And—I was sae left to mysel'—
   I sell't her an annuity.

The bargain lookit fair eneugh—
   She just was turn'd o' saxty-three—
I couldna guess'd she'd prove sae teugh,
   By human ingenuity.
But years have come, and years have gane,
And there she's yet as stieve's a stane—
The limmer's growin' young again,
   Since she got her annuity.

She's crined awa' to bane an' skin;
   But that, it seems, is nought to me:
She's like to live—although she's in
   The last stage o' tenuity.
She munches wi' her wizen'd gums,
An' stumps about on legs o' thrums,

But comes—as sure as Christmas comes—
To ca' for her annuity.

I read the tables drawn wi' care
For an Insurance Company;
Her chance o' life was stated there
Wi' perfect perspicuity.
But tables here or tables there,
She's lived ten years beyond her share,
An's like to live a dozen mair,
To ca' for her annuity.

Last Yule she had a fearfu' hoast—
I thought a kink might set me free—
I led her out 'mang snaw and frost,
Wi' constant assiduity.
But deil ma' care—the blast gaed by,
And miss'd the auld anatomy;
It just cost me a tooth, forbye
Discharging her annuity.

If there's a sough o' cholera
Or typhus—wha sae gleg as she!
She buys up baths, an' drugs, an' a',
In siccan superfluity!
She doesna need—she's fever proof—
The pest walk'd o'er her very roof—
She tauld me sae—an' then her loof
Held out for her annuity.

Ae day she fell—her arm she brak—
A compound fracture as could be—
Nae leech the cure wad undertak,
Whate'er was the gratuity.
It's cured!—She handles't like a flail—
It does as weel in bits as hale—
But I'm a broken man mysel'
Wi' her and her annuity.

Her broozled flesh and broken banes
 Are weel as flesh and banes can be.
She beats the taeds that live in stanes,
 An' fatten in vacuity!
They die when they're exposed to air—
They canna thole the atmosphere;
But her!—expose her onywhere—
 She lives for her annuity.

If mortal means could nick her thread,
 Sma' crime it wad appear to me—
Ca 't murder, or ca 't homicide—
 I'd justify 't—an' do it tae.
But how to fell a wither'd wife
That 's carved out o' the tree o' life—
The timmer limmer daurs the knife
 To settle her annuity.

I 'll try a shot.   But whar 's the mark?—
 Her vital parts are hid frae me.
Her back-bane wanders through her sark
 In an unkenn'd corkscrewity.
She 's palsified, an' shakes her head
Sae fast about, ye scarce can see 't—
It 's past the power o' steel or lead
 To settle her annuity.

She might be drown'd;—but go she'll not
 Within a mile o' loch or sea;—
Or hang'd—if cord could grip a throat
 O' siccan exiguity.
It 's fitter far to hang the rope—
It draws out like a telescope—
'Twad tak' a dreadfu' length o' drop
 To settle her annuity.

Will poison do 't?   It has been tried.
 But, be 't in hash or fricassee,

That's just the dish she can't abide,
  Whatever kind o' *gout* it ha'e.
It's needless to assail her doubts—
She gangs by instinct,—like the brutes,—
An' only eats an' drinks what suits
  Hersel' and her annuity.

The Bible says the age o' man
  Threescore and ten perchance may be.
She's ninety-four.   Let them wha can
  Explain the incongruity.
She should ha'e lived afore the flood—
She's come o' Patriarchal blood—
She's some auld Pagan mummified
  Alive for her annuity.

She's been embalm'd inside and out—
  She's sauted to the last degree—
There's pickle in her very snout
  Sae caper-like an' cruety,
Lot's wife was fresh compared to her—
They've Kyanized the useless knir—
She canna decompose—nae mair
  Than her accursed annuity.

The water-drap wears out the rock
  As this eternal jaud wears me.
I could withstand the single shock,
  But not the continuity.
It's pay me here—an' pay me there—
An' pay me, pay me, evermair—
I'll gang demented wi' despair—
  I'm *charged* for her annuity.

E

THE FATE OF BURNS.

By Thomas Carlyle.

CONTEMPLATING the sad end of Burns,—how he sank unaided by any real help, uncheered by any wise sympathy,—generous minds have sometimes figured to themselves, with a reproachful sorrow, that much might have been done for him; that, by counsel, true affection, and friendly ministrations, he might have been saved to himself and the world. But it seems dubious whether the richest, wisest, most benevolent individual could have lent Burns any effectual help.

Counsel—which seldom profits any one—he did not need. In his understanding, he knew the right from the wrong, as well, perhaps, as any man ever did; but the persuasion which would have availed him lies not so much in the head as in the heart, where no argument or expostulation could have assisted much to implant it.

As to money, we do not believe that this was his essential want; or well see that any private man could have bestowed on him an independent fortune, with much prospect of decisive advantage. It is a mortifying truth, that two men, in any rank of society, can hardly be found virtuous enough to give money, and to take it as a necessary gift, without an injury to the moral entireness of one or both. But so stands the fact:— Friendship, in the old heroic sense of the term, no longer exists; it is in reality no longer expected, or recognized as a virtue among men. A close observer of manners has pronounced "patronage"—that is, pecuniary or economic furtherance—to be "twice cursed;" cursing him that gives and him that takes! And thus, in regard to outward matters, it has become the rule, as, in regard to inward, it always was and must be the rule, that no one shall look for effectual help to another; but that each shall rest contented with what help he can afford himself. Such is the principle of modern Honour; naturally enough growing out of the sentiment of Pride, which we inculcate and encourage as the basis of our whole social morality.

We have already stated our doubts whether direct pecuniary help, had it been offered, would have been accepted, or could have proved very effectual. We shall readily admit, however, that much was to be done for Burns; that many a poisoned arrow might have been warded from his bosom; many an entanglement in his path cut asunder by the hand of the powerful; light and heat, shed on him from high places, would have made his humble atmosphere more genial; and the softest heart then breathing might have lived and died with fewer pangs. Still, we do not think that the blame of Burns's failure lies chiefly with the world. The world, it seems to us, treated him with more, rather than with less kindness than it usually shows to such men. It has ever, we fear, shown but small favour to its teachers: hunger and nakedness, perils and reviling, the prison, the poison-chalice, the cross, have, in most times and countries, been the market-price it has offered for wisdom —the welcome with which it has treated those who have come to enlighten and purify it. Homer and Socrates, and the Christian Apostles, belong to old days; but the world's martyrology was not completed with these. So neglected, so "persecuted they the prophets," not in

Judea only, but in all places where men have been. We reckon that every poet of Burns's order is, or should be, a prophet and teacher to his age; that he has no right to expect kindness, but rather is bound to do it; that Burns, in particular, experienced fully the usual proportion of goodness; and that the blame of his failure, as we have said, lies not chiefly with the world.

Where, then, does it lie? We are forced to answer, WITH HIMSELF: it is his inward, not his outward misfortunes, that bring him to the dust. Seldom, indeed, is it otherwise; seldom is a life morally wrecked, but the grand cause lies in some internal mal-arrangement,—some want, less of good fortune than of good guidance. Nature fashions no creature without implanting in it the strength needful for its action and duration; least of all does she neglect her master-piece and darling—the poetic soul! Neither can we believe that it is in the power of any external circumstances utterly to ruin the mind of a man; nay—if proper wisdom be given him—even so much as to affect its essential health and beauty. The sternest sum-total of all worldly misfortunes is death; nothing more can lie in the cup of human woe: yet many men, in all ages, have triumphed over death, and led it captive; converting its physical victory into a moral victory for themselves—into a seal and immortal consecration for all that their past life had achieved. What has been done may be done again; nay, it is but the degree, and not the kind, of such heroism, that differs in different seasons: for, without some portion of this spirit, not of boisterous daring, but of silent fearlessness —of SELF-DENIAL in all its forms, no great man, in any scene or time, has ever attained to be good.

By permission of Messrs. Chapman & Hall.

THE HUMOURS OF GLASGOW FAIR.

Oн, the sun frae the eastward was peeping,
  And braid through the winnocks did stare,
When Willie cried—" Tam are you sleeping?
  Mak' haste, man, and rise to the fair;
For the lads and lasses are thranging,
  And a' body's now in a steer;
Fye, haste ye, and let us be ganging,
  Or, faith, we'll be langsome I fear."

Then Tam he got up in a hurry,
  And wow but he made himsel' snod,
For a pint o' milk brose he did worry,
  To mak' him mair teuch for the road.
On his head his blue bonnet he slippet,
  His whip o'er his shouther he flang,
And a clumsy oak cudgel he grippet,
  On purpose the loons for to bang.

Now Willock had trysted wi' Jenny,
  For she was a braw canty queen;
Word gaed she had a gay penny,
  For whilk Willie fondly did green.
Now Tam he was blaming the liquor,
  Ae night he had got himsel' fou,
And trysted gleed Maggie MacVicar,
  And faith he thought shame for to rue.

The carles, fu' codgie, sat cocking
  Upon their white nags and their brown;
Wi' snuffing, and laughing, and joking,
  They soon canter'd into the town.

'Twas there was the funning and sporting—
Eh ! what a swarm o' braw folk—
Rowly powly, wild beasts, wheels o' fortune,
Sweety stan's, Master Punch, and Black Jock.

Now Willock and Tam, geyan bouzy,
By this time had met with their joes,
Consented wi' Gibbie and Susy
To gang awa' down to the shows.
'Twas there was the fiddling and drumming,
Sic a crowd, they could scarcely get through,
Fiddles, trumpets, and organs a' bumming;
O, sirs, what a hully baloo.

Then hie to the tents at the paling,
Weel theekit wi' blankets and mats,
And deals seated round like a tap-room,
Supported on stanes and on pats.
The whisky like water they're selling,
And porter as sma' as their yill,—
And aye as ye're pouring they're telling,
" Troth, dear, it 's just sixpence the gill ! "

Says Meg—" See yon beast wi' the claes on 't,
Wi' the face o 't as black as the soot;
Preserve 's ! it has fingers and taes on 't—
Eh, lass, it 's an unco like brute ! "
" O, woman, but ye are a gomeral,
To mak' sic a won'er at that,
D'ye na ken, daft gowk, that 's a mongrel,
That 's bred 'twixt a dog and a cat.

" See yon supple jade how she 's dancing,
Wi' the white ruffled breeks and red shoon,
Frae tap to the tae she 's a glancing,
Wi' gowd, and a feather aboon,—

My troth, she's a braw decent kimmer
As I have yet seen in the fair."
" Her decent !" quo' Meg, " she's some limmer,
Or, faith, she would never be there."

Now Gibbie was wanting a toothfu'—
Says he, " I 'm right tired o' the fun,
D'ye think we 'd be the waur o' a mouthfu'
O' gude nappy yill and a bun ? "
" Wi' a' my heart," says Tam, " feth I 'm willing,—
'Tis best to water the corn;
By jing, I 've a bonny white shilling,
And a saxpence that ne'er saw the morn."

Before they got out o' the bustle,
Poor Tam got his fairing, I trow,
For a stick at the ging'bread played whistle,
And knocked him down like a cow.
Says Tam,—" Wha did that ? deil confound them,—
Fair play, let me win at the loon ;
And he whirled his stick round and round him,
And swore like a very dragoon.

Then next for a house they gaed glow'ring,
Whare they might get wetting their mou'.
Says Meg—" Here's a house keeps a pouring,
Wi' the sign o' the muckle black cow."
" A cow !" quo' Jenny, " ye gawky,
Preserve us ! but ye 've little skill;
Ye haveral, did ye e'er see a hawky
Like that—look again and ye'll see its a *bill*."

But just as they darken'd the entry,
Says Willie—" We 're now far eneugh,
I see its a house for the gentry,—
Let 's gang to the sign o' the Pleuch."

"Na, faith," says Gibbie, "we'se better
    Gae dauner to auld Luckie Gunn's;
For there I 'm to meet wi' my father,
    And auld uncle Jock o' the Whins."

Now they a' in Luckie's had landed,
    Twa rounds at the bicker to try;
The whisky and yill round was handed,
    And baps in great bourocks did lie.
Blind Alick, the fiddler, was trysted,
    And he was to handle the bow;
On a big barrel-head he was hoisted,
    To keep himsel' out o' the row.

Had ye seen sic a din and gafaaing,
    Sic hooching and dancing was there;
Sic rugging, and riving, and drawing,
    Was ne'er seen before in a fair.
For Tam, he wi' Maggie was wheeling,
    And he gied sic a terrible loup,
That his head cam' a thump on the ceiling,
    And he cam' down wi' a dump on his doup.

Now they ate and they drank till their bellies
    Were bent like the head o' a drum;
Syne they raise, and they caper'd like fillies,
    Whene'er that the fiddle played bum.
Wi' dancing they now were grown weary,
    And scarcely were able to stan',
So they took to the road a' fu' cheery,
    As day was beginning to dawn.

THE SHEPHERD AS M.P. FOR THE GUSE-DUBS.

BY PROFESSOR WILSON.

Shepherd. I wad prefer sitting for the Guse-dubs * o Glasgow. O, sirs! what a huddle o' houses, and what a hubbub o'——

North. Gently, James, gently—Your love of allitera‑ tion allures you occasionally across the confines of coarseness, and——

Shepherd. If you interrup me, Mr. North, I 'll no scruple to interrup you, in spite o' a' my respect for your age and endowments. But was ye ever in the Guse-dubs o' Glasgow? Safe us a'! what clarty closses, narrowin' awa' and darkenin' doun—some stracht, and some serpentine —into green middens o' baith liquid and solid matter, soomin' wi' dead cats and auld shoon, and rags o' petti‑ coats that had been worn till they fell aff and wad wear nae langer; and then ayont the midden, or say, rather surrounding the great central stagnant flood o' fulzie, the windows o' a coort, for a coort they ca 't, some wi' panes o' glass and panes o' paper time about, some wi' what had ance been a hat in this hole, and what had been a pair o' breeks in that hole, and some without lozens a' thegither; and then siccan fierce faces o' lads that had enlisted, and were keeping themselves drunk night and day on the bounty-money, before ordered to join the regiment in the Wast Indies, and die o' the yallow fever! And what fearsome faces o' limmers, like

* A low locality in Glasgow.

she-demons dragging them down into debauchery, and
hauding them there, as in a vice, when they ha'e gotten
them down,—and, wad ye believe 't, swearin' and dammin
ane anither's een, and then lauchin', and tryin' to look
lo'esome, and jeerin' and leerin' like Jezabels.

Tickler. Hear! hear! hear!

Shepherd. Dive down anither close, and you hear a
man murderin' his wife, upstairs in a garret. A' at ance
flees open the door at the stair-head, and the mutchless
mawsey, a' dreepin' wi' bluid, flings herself frae the tap
step o' the flicht to the causeway, and into the nearest
change-house, roaring in rage and terror—twa emotions
that are no canny when they chance to forgather—and
ca'in for a constable to tak' haud o' her gudeman, who
has threatened to ding out her brains wi' a hammer, or
cut her throat wi' a razor.

North. What painting, Tickler! What a Salvator is
our Shepherd!

Shepherd. Down anither close, and a battle o' dowgs!
A bull-dowg and a mastiff! The great big brown mastiff
mouthin' the bull-dowg by the verra hainches, as if to
crunch his back, and the wee white bull-dowg never
seemin' to fash his thoomb, but stickin' by the regular
set teeth o' his under-hung jaw to the throat o' the
mastiff, close to the jugular, and no to be drawn aff the
grip by twa strong baker-boys pu'in at the tail o' the
tane, and twa strong butcher-boys pu'in at the tail o'
the tither—for the mastiff's maister begins to fear that the
veeper at his throat will kill him outright, and offers to
pay a' betts and confess his dowg has lost the battle.
But the crood wush to see the fecht out—and harl the
dowgs that are noo worryin' ither without ony growlin'—

baith silent, except a sort o' snortin' through the nostrils and a kind o' guller in their gullets—I say, the crood harl them out o' the midden, ontil the stanes again—and "Weel dune, Cæsar." "Better dune, Veeper." "A mutchkin to a gill on Whitey." "The muckle ane canna fecht." "See how the wee bick is worryin' him now, by a new spat on the thrapple." "He wad rin awa' gin she wad let him loose." "She's just like her mither that belanged to the caravan o' wild beasts." "Oh man, Davie, but I wad like to get a breed out o' her, by the watch-dowg at Bell-meadow bleachfield, that killed, ye ken, the Kilmarnock carrier's Help in twunty minutes, at Kingswell"——

North. I never heard you speak in such kind before, James——

Shepherd. I'm describing the character o' my constituents, you ken, and should be eloquent, for you will recollec' that I sat out wi' imagining mysel Member o' Parliament, that is representative o' the Guse-dubs. But, as Horace says,—

"Est modus in rebus, sunt certi denique fines."

I crave a bumper. Faith claret's no that strong, so I'll drink the toast this time in a tummler,—"Baith sides o' the Tweed!"—Hip—hip—hip—hurraw! After a', I maun confess that I like the Englishers, if they wadna be sae pernicketty * about what they eat.

* "Pernicketty,"—Particular.

A BALLAD OF BANNOCKBURN.

BY J. B. MANSON.

I.

O FOR a gush of Castaly
  To undulate my song,
Ye goddess-muses, unto whom
  The springs of verse belong! . . .
No matter, there are streams enow
  Between the hill and sea,
And every Scot's foot on their banks,
  Thanks to King Bruce, is free.

II.

The English King has sworn an oath
  That, ere the Baptist's Day,
Near Stirling's towers shall England's host
  And Scotland's meet in fray;
Such fray as, if it lifts us not
  Above all fear and praise,
Shall be the last and bloodiest
  Of Scotland's fighting days.

III.

To cot, to castle spread the news,
  O'er hill, dale, everywhere;
It found God-speed in Liddesdale,
  It found God-speed in Ayr;
Among the mosses of Dumfries
  The Maxwells caught the omen;
Buchanan passed it to Colquhoun
  In the shadow of Ben Lomond;

'Twas heard at Ebba's Kirk, and heard
  By them that hear the din
Of Corryvreckan, and Cape Wrath,
  And Foyers, and Corra Linn.
It spread, it sprang through isle to isle
  From Harris to Tyree;
It roused the red-legged clans of Ross
  And the Dane-mixed men of Dee;
It pierced beyond the springs of Clyde
  And the virgin-rill of Spey;
It woke the country of St. Clair
  And the country of Mackay;
It coursed the shealings of the Tay
  From Gowrie to Glen Lyon;
It reached the shaggy clans whose boats
  Were rocking on Loch Ryan,
Till every heady chief blazed up
  In wildest Galloway,
Where the relics of Saint Ninian sleep
  And the monks of Baliol pray.
Our misty glens became like hives
  When swarming time is come,
And the grim glensmen felt their blood
  Too hot to stay at home.
The fasting huntsman left the track
  Of deer already stricken;
Even in the lazy bedesman's veins
  It made a new life quicken.
Proud mothers ceased to sing, I trow,
  And maidens to be coy,   .
But the warrior heard it and ground his teeth
  And cut the air for joy!

IV.

On Bannock's bank there lies a fen,
  The nurse of cold and fog,
The orchis blows, the mire-snipe goes,
  At will o'er Milton Bog.

To cross this faithless fen, thou may'st
  Man's foot for years defy,
But now—so hot the breath of June—
  The faithless fen was dry;
Though happily the northern bank
  Rose rugged, steep, and high.
King Bruce look'd round and chose his ground;
  "Now let the foe," said he,
"But meet me here, I shall not fear
  To face him—one to three."

V.

'Twas now full tide of summer-shine
  And near the Baptist's Day,
But nearer yet the stately stretch
  Of Edward's proud array.
Already he had cool'd his steed
  In Carron's fatal flood,
Already had his trumpets broke
  The silence of Torwood;
From Camelon on to Dunipace,
  And farther on to Plean,
Few were the hinds he found at home
  To bid him hail, I ween.

VI.

And, sooth, it was a proud array
  Came rolling o'er the heights,
With all the bravest of his realm
  And knightliest of his knights;
Such lords as Pembroke's baron bold,
  Such knights as D'Argentine,
And Gloster's Earl and Hereford's,
  Who led the foremost line.
Their burnish'd mail and twinkling blades
  Made all the land ablaze,
And all the sky was fringed with flags
  For two long summer days.

VII.

The men-at-arms came prancing up
  With loud and saucy jeers;
Few men-at-arms had we, but show'd
  A hedge of trusty spears.
That hedge of ashen spears 'twas said,
  Made even De Valence pause:
" Perdie!" he said, " yon catamount
  Hath little lack of claws."

VIII.

In battles four the Scots are ranked,
  Their King the guiding soul,
That gives to each its fit behest,
  And oneness to the whole.
Lord Randolph shakes his border spear
  All in the middle fight,
And James the Douglas holds the left,
  And Edward Bruce the right;
While Keith the Marshall hangs in wait
  Behind on Bannock's bank,
With good five hundred horse to take
  The English bows in flank.

IX.

The day that makes each week arise
  With the blue eye of heaven,
It found us on the battle-field
  But not to arms was given;
Yet not to rest, or hope of rest,
  With the broad sun blazing o'er us,
And a hundred thousand English swords
  Gathering before us.
That day the sun went down like blood
  And e'en when rose the moon,
All the night air palpitated
  With the fiery heart of June,

X.

That day, 'twas said, the sky had signs
　Which none but sages see,
But on the earth were omens too
　Fill'd all our hearts with glee.
We saw our good King's battle-axe
　Crash through De Bohun's brain;
We saw the English braggart's corpse
　Fall to the ground in twain;
And the proud sound of mastery
　Rose swelling on our rear,
Where gallant D'Aynecourt gave his blood
　To Randolph's border spear.

XI.

Sir Mowbray stood in chafing mood
　On Stirling's old grey wall,
For nought on earth had he to do
　But watch our movements all.
And well he noted every sign, —
　" The time," quoth he, " is brief,
When yonder nodding flags, my boys,
　Shall bring us all relief.
Another day, one bloody fray,"
　Quoth he, " and I am free;
The mouse may cheep in Stirling keep,
　But not, please God, for me."

XII.

Sir Mowbray was a gallant knight
　And raised to high command
By the great soul that left his clay
　At Borough-on-the-Sand.
And give the old knight his wonted place
　Among the Southerns hot,
And let him tread the living sward,
　In teeth of the proud Scot,

That arm of his has pith enough
  To show you lion's play,
Where the fire flies from flashing eyes,
  The blue eyes and the grey!

XIII.

Next morn arose as peaceful
  As if war had never been,
Though nations twain in battle-gear
  Were standing in its sheen,
With gilded flags, like Beltane fires,
  All gleaming in the sun,
And men on both sides muttering "Thus
  Shall battle-fields be won!"

XIV.

Like waters fed by numerous springs
  The Northern ranks are throng'd
With vassal leal and bold outlaw,
  The wronger and the wrong'd;
Grim grey-beards that have swung their swords
  Around the Wallace wight;
Brave striplings that have fled from home,
  But will not flee from fight;
And some who have aforetime fought
  Against the leal and true,
Will this day stand in Scotland's van
  And soldier penance do;
Yea, even the knave whose caitiff-life
  Has hardly one proud day,
Who comes to plunder—he for once
  Has come in time to slay.

XV.

King Bruce surveyed his motley host
  With no unhopeful eye;
"Let every soldier make his bed
  As he would wish to lie!
F

I give Old Scotland's flag in charge
  To this grey rock," said he,—
" A standard-bearer that shall fly,
  Good friends, as soon as we!"

XVI.

Our gracious King!   Right well we knew
  How he had played the man,
How he had lived an outlaw's life,
  And borne the Church's ban,
And how he kept his fame so well
  In flight when doomed to flee,
And how he nurs'd a heart of ruth
  In the breast of victory!
Ho, for the men that loved their King,
  When loyal men were few!
Ho, for the King that knew his men
  And trusted whom he knew!
And, Scotsmen, sacred keep that stone
  Till Bannock Burn runs dry,
For from that stone our stainless flag,
  And not one Scot, did fly.

XVII.

Old Maurice of Inchaffray
  (Save his grey head from harm!)
Had brought to bless our battle-field
  Saint Fillan's relic arm;
But how our hearts beat in us,
  When we heard the good man say,
That living arms, and laymen nerves,
  Were all required to-day!
And when he raised the Cross, and bade
  Us cry unto the Lord,
And seek the grace of every saint
  That ever drew a sword,

And pardon'd fight, and pardon'd fall—
  Scarce was the counsel given,
When hand to heart, and knee to earth,
  And every eye to heaven:
Ye could have heard the Abbot tread,
  Unsandall'd though he trod,
So breathlessly the Scottish host
  Were crying to their God !
"They kneel," exclaimed the Southern King
  "For grace the traitors sue."
"They sue for grace," said Umfraville,
  "But not my liege, from you!"

XVIII.

Now came proud England's battle-burst.—
  O ladies, 'twere a sight
On which the fairest ladye-eye
  With joyaunce would alight,
To see such gallant gentlemen
  At tourney, dance, or play;
But this was not the time of feast,
  Or joust, or holiday!

XIX.

And first the cloud of archery
  Threw out its arrowy sleet—
God help the doom'd but dauntless breasts
  On whom that shower did beat !
But Keith has rounded Milton Bog,
  On Bannock's farthest bank,
And with a fair five hundred horse
  Dash'd right into their flank.
Ten thousand strong, the bowmen stood,
  All train'd to bend the yew.
But with his fair five hundred
  The Keith has bit them through.

XX.

Then Scotland bared her good broadsword
　And baptized it in blood,
And Bannock Burn was swollen and red,
　But not with rain or mud.
And when the men-at-arms assay'd
　Our bristling hedge of ash,
'Twas such a crash of spears that men
　For miles could hear the crash.

XXI.

Even the base followers of the camp,
　Debarred the grace of fight,
No sooner heard the crash of spears
　Than they, too, came in sight;
Came trooping up the weather-gleam
　And fringed the Gillies' Hill,
Arriving like a fresher force
　To chase, if not to kill.
"A second host!" King Edward cried,
　" And mine is almost gone!"
"Nay, sire," De Valence said, "the Scots
　To-day will need but one."

XXII.

For each man fought as boors might work
　In harvest-time or spring,—
'Twas the spring-time of liberty,
　But hate's in-gathering,—
Till on the uneven and pitted ground,
　With caltrops thickly sown,
A crop of staggering cavaliers
　And plunging steeds was mown;
Till Hereford had turned his rein,
　Till Gloster's heart was cold,
(Brave Gloster's death-bed shall be call'd
　For aye the Bloody Fold),—

Till knightly D'Argentine, had urged
   The Southern King away,
Brave D'Argentine, whose one good sword
   Almost renewed the fray!
Till home-fast boys and screaming girls
   Beheld, at Ingram's Crook,
Balls of red foam and trunkless heads
   Slow sailing down the brook!
The very winds were vocal,
   And the dumb hills seem'd to cry,
" Your bairns are sleeping at our feet,
   Ho! save your homes or die."
And saved they were, and safe they are,
   And shall be safe and free,
For Right was Might at Bannock Burn—
   To God all glory be!

XXIII.

That night by Ninian's sleepless monks
   Many a prayer was said;
That night the trophied tidings brought
   Sweet dreams to wife and maid;
That night we bound the wounded up,
   To-morrow hid the slain;
One short hour reckon'd up our loss,—
   All time shall count the gain.
For 'tis a story to be held
   In memory for aye,
How lord and vassal knelt and pray'd—
   Though not as bedesmen pray,
How lord and vassal rose and fought
   As ne'er was fought before,
And how the burn was choked with knights,
   And the marsh half-fill'd with gore,
And how the Northern Sun arose
   As sank the Southern Star,
And how the braggart Southern King
   Did ride to reach Dunbar!

XXIV.

O luckless, luckless King, that broke
The barb of Edward's name!
O starless breast, that came so far
And found so little fame!
Ah, well for thee hadst thou been left
With Gloster on the plain!
Thou go'st to gall a noble steed,
A steed thou canst not rein.
Thou go'st—O luckless, luckless King!—
To Favouritism's foul breath,
To trust a courtier's puny arm,
To Berkeley's horrid death!
And England's wide and motley realm
Holds not so poor a thing
As thine anointed, witless head,
O, luckless, luckless king!

By permission.

SCOTCH WORDS.

By the late Robert Leighton.

They speak in riddles north beyond the Tweed.
The plain, pure English they can deftly read;
Yet when without the book they come to speak,
Their lingo seems half English and half Greek.

Their jaws are *chafts;* their hands when closed are *neives;*
Their bread 's not cut in slices, but in *sheives;*
Their armpits are their *oxters;* palms are *luifs;*
Their men are *chields;* their timid fools are *cuiffs;*
Their lads are *callants,* and their women *kimmers;*
Good lassies *denty queans,* and bad ones *limmers.*
They *thole* when they endure, *scart* when they scratch;
And when they give a sample it 's a *swatch.*

* From *The Bapteezment o' the Bairn,* &c. ; J. Menzies & Co., Edinburgh.

Scolding is *flytin'*, and a long palaver
Is nothing but a *blether* or a *haver.*
This room they call the *but*, and that the *ben;*
And what they do not know they *dinna ken.*
On keen cold days they say the wind *blaws snell.*
And when they wipe their nose they *dicht* their *byke;*
And they have words that Johnson could not spell,
As *umph'm*, which means—anything you like:
While some, though purely English, and well known,
Have yet a Scottish meaning of their own:—
To *prig's* to plead, beat down a thing in cost;
To *coff's* to purchase, and a cough's a *host;*
To *crack* is to converse; the *lift's* the sky;
And *bairns* are said to *greet* when children cry.
When lost, folk never ask the way they want—
They *speir* the *gate;* and when they yawn they *gaunt.*
Beetle with them is *clock;* a flame's a *lowe;*
Their straw is *strae;* chaff *cauff*, and hollow, *howe;*
A *pickle* means a few; *muckle* is big;
And a piece of crockeryware is called a *pig.*

Speaking of pigs—when Lady Delacour
Was on her celebrated Scottish tour,
One night she made her quarters at the "Crown,"
The head inn of a well-known county town.
The chambermaid, on lighting her to bed,
Before withdrawing, curtsied low, and said,—

"This nicht is cauld, my leddy, wad ye please,
To hae a pig i' the bed to warm your taes!"

"A pig in bed to tease!   What's that you say?
You are impertinent—away, away!"

"Me impudent! no, mem—I meant nae harm,
But just the greybeard pig to keep ye warm."

"Insolent hussy, to confront me so !
This very instant shall your mistress know.
The bell—there's none, of course—go, send her here."

"My mistress, mem, I dinna need to fear:
In sooth, it was hersel' that bade me speir.
Nae insult, mem; we thocht ye wad be gled,
On this cauld nicht, to hae a pig i' the bed."

"Stay, girl; your words are strangely out of place,
And yet I see no insult in your face.
Is it a custom in your country, then,
For ladies to have pigs in bed wi' them?"

"Oh, quite a custom wi' the gentles, mem;
Wi' gentle ladies, ay, and gentle men;
And, troth, if single, they wad sairly miss
Their het pig on a cauldrif nicht like this."

"I've seen strange countries—but this surely beats
Their rudest makeshift for a warming pan.
Suppose, my girl, I should adopt your plan,
You would not put the pig between the sheets?"

"Surely, my leddy, and nae itherwhere:
Please, mem, ye'll find it do the maist guid there."

"Fie, fie, 'twould dirty them, and if I keep
In fear of that, you know, I shall not sleep."

"Ye'll sleep far better, mem.   Tak' my advice;
The nicht blaws snell—the sheets are cauld as ice;
I'll fetch you up a fine, warm, cozy pig;
I'll mak' ye sae comfortable and trig,
Wi' coortains, blankets, every kind o' hap,
And warrant ye to sleep as sound's a tap.
As for the fylin' o' the sheets—dear me,
The pig's as clean outside as pig can be.

A weel-closed mooth's eneuch for ither folk,
But if you like, I'll put it in a poke."

"But, Effie—that's your name, I think you said—
Do you yourself, now, take a pig to bed?"

"Eh! na, mem, pigs are only for the great,
Wha lie on feather beds, and sit up late.
Feathers and pigs are no for puir riff-raff—
Me and my neibour lassie lie on cauff."

"What's that—a calf!   If I your sense can gather,
You and the other lassie sleep together—
Two in a bed, and with the calf between ;
That, I suppose, my girl, is what you mean?"

"Na, na, my leddy—'od ye're jokin' noo—
We sleep thegither, that is very true—
But nocht between us : wi' our claes all aff,
Except our sarks, we lie *upon* the cauff."

"Well, well, my girl! I am surprised to hear
That we of English habits live so near
Such barbarous customs.—Effie, you may go :
As for the pig, I thank you, but—no, no—
Ha, ha! good night—excuse me if I laugh—
I'd rather be without both pig and calf."

    On the return of Lady Delacour,
She wrote a book about her northern tour,
Wherein the facts are graphically told,
That Scottish gentlefolks, when nights are cold,
Take into bed fat pigs to keep them warm ;
While common folk, who share their beds in halves—
Denied the richer comforts of the farm—
Can only warm their sheets with lean, cheap calves.
                              By permission of Mrs. Leighton.

A TALE OF PENTLAND.

By James Hogg, "The Ettrick Shepherd."

Mr. John Haliday having been in hiding on the hills, after the battle of Pentland, became impatient to hear news concerning the sufferings of his brethren who had been in arms, and in particular if there were any troops scouring the district in which he had found shelter. Accordingly, he left his hiding-place in the evening, and travelled towards the valley until about midnight, when, coming to the house of Gabriel Johnstone, and perceiving a light, he determined on entering, as he knew him to be a devout man, and one much concerned about the sufferings of the Church of Scotland.

Mr. Haliday, however, approached the house with great caution, for he rather wondered why there should be a light there at midnight, while at the same time he neither heard psalms singing nor the accents of prayer. So casting off his heavy shoes, for fear of making a noise, he stole softly up to the little window from whence the light beamed, and peeped in, where he saw, not Johnstone, but another man, whom he did not know, in the very act of cutting a soldier's throat, while Johnstone's daughter, a comely girl, about twenty years of age, was standing deliberately by, and holding the candle to him.

Haliday was seized with an inexpressible terror; for the floor was all blood, and the man was struggling in

the agonies of death, and from his dress he appeared to
have been a cavalier of some distinction. So completely
was the Covenanter overcome with horror that he turned
and fled from the house with all his might. So much
had Haliday been confounded that he even forgot to lift
his shoes, but fled without them; and he had not run
above half a bowshot before he came upon two men
hastening to the house of Gabriel Johnstone. As soon
as they perceived him running towards them they fled,
and he pursued them, for when he saw them so ready to
take alarm, he was sure they were some of the persecuted
race, and tried eagerly to overtake them, exerting his
utmost speed, and calling on them to stop. All this
only made them run faster, and when they came to a.
feal-dyke they separated, and ran different ways, and he
soon thereafter lost sight of them both.

This house, where Johnstone lived, is said to have
been in a lonely concealed dell, not far from West
Linton, in what direction I do not know, but it was
towards that village that Haliday fled, not knowing
whither he went, till he came to the houses. Having
no acquaintances here whom he durst venture to
call up, and the morning having set in frosty, he began
to conceive that it was absolutely necessary for him to
return to the house of Gabriel Johnstone, and try to
regain his shoes, as he little knew when or where it
might be in his power to get another pair. Accordingly
he hasted back by a nearer path, and coming to the
place before it was day, found his shoes. At the same
time he heard a fierce contention within the house, but
as there seemed to be a watch he durst not approach it,
but again made his escape.

Having brought some victuals along with him, he did not return to his hiding-place that day, which was in a wild height, south of Biggar, but remained in the moss of Craigengaur; and as soon as it grew dark descended again into the valley. Again he perceived a light in the distance, where he thought no light should have been. But he went towards it, and as he approached he heard the melody of psalm-singing issuing from the place, and floating far on the still breeze of the night. He hurried to the spot, and found the reverend and devout Mr. Livingston, in the act of divine worship, in an old void barn on the lands of Slipperfield, with a great number of serious and pious people, who were all much affected both by his prayers and discourse.

After the worship was ended, Haliday made up to the minister, among many others, to congratulate him on the splendour of his discourse, and implore " a further supply of the same milk of redeeming grace, with which they found their souls nourished, cherished, and exalted." The good man complied with the request, and appointed another meeting at the same place on a future night.

Haliday having been formerly well acquainted with the preacher, convoyed him on his way home, where they condoled with one another on the hardness of their lots; and Haliday told him of the scene he had witnessed at the house of Gabriel Johnstone. The heart of the good minister was wrung with grief, and he deplored the madness and malice of the people who had committed an act that would bring down tenfold vengeance on the heads of the whole persecuted race. At length it was resolved between them that, as soon as it was day, they would go and reconnoitre, and if they found the case of the

aggravated nature they suspected, they would themselves be the first to expose it, and give the perpetrators
up to justice.

Accordingly, next morning they took another man into
the secret, a William Rankin, one of Mr. Livingston's
elders, and the three went away to Johnstone's house, to
investigate the case of the cavalier's murder; but there
was a guard of three armed men opposed them, and
neither promises, nor threatenings, nor all the minister's
eloquence, could induce them to give way one inch.
The men advised the intruders to take themselves off lest
a worse thing might befall them; and as they continued
to motion them away, with the most impatient gestures,
the kind divine and his associates thought meet to retire,
and leave the matter as it was; and thus was this
mysterious affair hushed up in silence and darkness for
that time, no tongue having been heard to mention it
further than as above recited. The three armed men
were all unknown to the others, but Haliday observed
that one of them was the very youth whom he saw cutting
off the soldier's head with a knife.

The rage and cruelty of the Popish party seemed to
gather new virulence every day, influencing all the counsels of the king; and the persecution of the non-
conformists was proportionably severe. One new act
of council was issued after another, all tending to root
the Covenanters out of Scotland, but it had only the
effect of making their tenets still dearer to them. The
longed-for night of the meeting in the old hay-barn at
length arrived, and it was attended by a still greater
number than on the night preceding. A more motley group
can hardly be conceived than appeared in the barn that

night, and the lamps being weak and dim, rendered the appearance of the assembly still more striking. It was, however, observed that about the middle of the service a number of fellows came in with broad slouch bonnets, and watch-coats or cloaks about them, who placed themselves in equal divisions at the two doors, and remained without uncovering their heads, two of them being busily engaged taking notes. Before Mr. Livingston began the last prayer, however, he desired the men to uncover, which they did, and the service went on to the end; but no sooner had the minister pronounced the word *Amen*, than the group of late comers threw off their cloaks, and drawing out swords and pistols, their commander, one General Drummond, charged the whole congregation in the king's name to surrender.

A scene of the utmost confusion ensued; the lights being extinguished, many of the young men burst through the roof of the old barn in every direction, and though many shots were fired at them in the dark, great numbers escaped; but Mr. Livingston and other eleven were retained prisoners, and conveyed to Edinburgh, where they were examined before the council and cast into prison. Among the prisoners was Mr. Haliday and the identical young man whom he had seen in the act of murdering the cavalier, and who turned out to be a Mr. John Lindsay, from Edinburgh, who had been at the battle of Pentland; and in hiding afterwards.

Great was the lamentation for the loss of Mr. Livingston, who was so highly esteemed by his hearers. The short extracts from his sermons in the barn, that were produced against him on his trial, prove him to have been a man endowed with talents somewhat above the greater part of his contemporaries. His text that night it appears had been taken from Genesis:—"And God saw the wickedness of man that it was great in the earth, and that every imagination of the thoughts of his heart was only evil continually." One of the quoted passages concludes thus:—

"Let us join together in breaking the bands of the oppressors, and casting their cords from us. As for myself, as a member of this poor persecuted Church of Scotland, and an unworthy minister of it, I hereby call upon you all, in the name of God, to set your faces, your hearts, and your hands against all such acts, which are or shall be passed against the covenanted work of reformation in this kingdom; that we here declare ourselves free of the guilt of them, and pray that God may put this in record in heaven."

These words having been sworn to, and Mr. Livingston not denying them, a sharp debate arose in the council what punishment to award. The king's advocate urged the utility of sending him forthwith to the gallows; but some friends in the council got his sentence commuted to banishment; and he was accordingly banished the kingdom. Six more, against whom nothing could be proven farther than their having been present at a conventicle, were sentenced to imprisonment for two months; among this number Haliday was one. The other five were condemned to be executed at the cross of Edinburgh, on the 14th of December following; and among this last unhappy number was Mr. John Lindsay.

Haliday now tried all the means he could devise to gain an interview with Lindsay, to have some explanation of the extraordinary scene he had witnessed in the cottage at midnight, for it had made a fearful impression upon his mind, and he never could get rid of it for a moment; having still in his mind's eye a beautiful country maiden standing with a pleased face, holding a candle, and Lindsay in the meantime at his horrid task. His endeavours, however, were all in vain, for they were in different prisons, and the jailer paid no attention to his requests. But there was a gentleman in the privy council that year, whose name, I think, was Gilmour, to whose candour Haliday conceived that both he and some of his associates owed their lives. To this gentleman, therefore, he applied by letter, requesting a private interview with him, as he had a singular instance of barbarity to communicate, which it would be well to inquire into while the possibility of doing so remained, for the access to it would soon be sealed for ever. The gentleman attended immediately, and Haliday revealed to him the circumstances previously mentioned, stating that the murderer now lay in the Tolbooth jail, under sentence of death.

Gilmour appeared much interested, as well as astonished at the narrative, and taking out a note-book, he looked over some dates, and then observed:—" This date of yours tallies exactly with one of my own, relating to an incident of the same sort, but the circumstances narrated are so different that I must conceive either that you are mistaken, or that you are trumping up this story to screen some other guilty person or persons."

Haliday disclaimed all such motives, and persevered in his attestations. Gilmour then took him along with him to the Tolbooth prison, where the two were admitted to a private interview with the prisoner, and there charged him with the crime of murder in such a place and on such a night; but he denied the whole with disdain. Haliday told him that it was in vain for him to deny it, for he beheld him in the very act of perpetrating the murder with his own eyes, while Gabriel Johnstone's daughter stood deliberately and held the candle to him.

" Hold your tongue, fellow!" said Lindsay, disdainfully, "for you know not what you are saying. What a cowardly dog you must be by your own account! If you saw me murdering a gentleman cavalier, why did you not rush in to his assistance?"

" I could not have saved the gentleman then," said Haliday, " and I thought it not meet to intermeddle in such a scene of blood."

" It was as well for you that you did not," said Lindsay.

" Then you acknowledge being in the cottage of the dell that night?" said Gilmour.

" And if I was what is that to you? Or what is it now to me or any person? I *was* there on the night specified; but I am ashamed of the part I there acted, and am now well requited for it. Yes, requited as I ought to be, so let it rest; for not one syllable of the transaction shall any one hear from me."

Thus they were obliged to leave the prisoner, and forthwith Gilmour led Haliday up a stair to a lodging in the Parliament Square, where they found a gentleman lying sick in bed, to whom Mr. Gilmour said, after inquiring after his health, " Brother Robert, I conceive that we two have found out the young man who saved your life at the cottage among the' mountains."

"I would give the half that I possess that this were true," said the sick gentleman; " who or where is he?"

"If I am right in my conjecture," said the privy councillor, "he is lying in the Tolbooth jail, there under sentence of death, and has but a few days to live. But tell me, brother, could you know him, or have you any recollection of his appearance?"

"Alas! I have none!" said the other, mournfully, "for I was insensible, through the loss of blood, the whole time I was under his protection; and if I ever heard his name I have lost it, the whole of that period being a total blank in my memory. But he must be a hero of the first rank; and therefore, oh, my dear brother, save him whatever his crime may be."

"His life is justly forfeited to the laws of his country, brother," said Gilmour, "and he must die with the rest."

"He shall not die with the rest, if I should die for him," cried the sick man vehemently: "I will move heaven and earth before my brave deliverer shall die like a felon."

"Calm yourself, brother, and trust that part to me," said Gilmour. "I think my influence saved the life of this gentleman, as well as the lives of some others; and it was all on account of the feeling of respect I had for the party, one of whom, or rather two of whom, acted such a noble and distinguished part toward you. But pray, undeceive this gentleman by narrating the facts to him, in which he cannot miss to be interested." The sick man, whose name it seems, if I remember aright, was Captain Robert Gilmour, of the volunteers, then proceeded as follows:—

"There having been high rewards offered for the apprehension of some south-country gentlemen, whose correspondence with Mr. Welch, and some other of the

fanatics, had been intercepted, I took advantage of
information I obtained regarding the place of their
retreat, and set out, certain of apprehending two of them
at least.

"Accordingly I went off one morning about the
beginning of November, with only five followers, well
armed and mounted. We left Gilmerton long before it
was light, and having a trusty guide, rode straight to their
hiding-place, where we did not arrive till towards the
evening, when we started them. They were seven in
number, and were armed with swords and bludgeons;
but, being apprized of our approach, they fled from us,
and took shelter in a morass, into which it was impossible
to follow them on horseback. But perceiving three
more men on another hill, I thought there was no
time to lose, so giving one of my men our horses to hold,
the rest of us advanced into the morass with drawn swords
and loaded horse pistols. I called to them to surrender,
but they stood upon their guard, determined on resistance;
and just while we were involved to the knees in the mire
of the morass, they broke in upon us, pell-mell, and for
about two minutes the engagement was very sharp.
There was an old man struck me a terrible blow with
a bludgeon, and was just about to repeat it when I
brought him down with a shot from my pistol. A young
fellow then ran at me with his sword; and as I still stuck
in the moss, I could not ward the blow, so that he got a
fair stroke at my neck, meaning, without doubt, to cut
off my head; and he would have done it had his sword
been sharp. As it was, he cut it to the bone, and opened
one of the jugular veins. I fell; but my men firing a
volley in their faces, at that moment, they fled. It

seems we did the same, without loss of time; for I must now take my narrative from the report of others, as I remember no more that passed. My men bore me on their arms to our horses, and then mounted and fled, trying all that they could to stanch the bleeding of my wound. But perceiving a party coming down a hill, as with the intent of cutting off their retreat, and losing all hopes of saving my life, they carried me into a cottage in a wild lonely retreat, commended me to the care of the inmates, and after telling them my name, and in what manner I received my death-wound, they thought proper to provide for their own safety, and so escaped.

"The only inmates of that lonely house, at least at that present time, were a lover and his mistress, both intercommuned Whigs; and when my men left me on the floor, the blood, which they had hitherto restrained in part, burst out afresh and deluged the floor. The young man said it was best to put me out of pain; but the girl wept and prayed him rather to render me some assistance. 'O Johnny, man, how can you speak that gate?' cried she; 'suppose he be our mortal enemy, he is aye ane o' God's creatures, an' has a soul to be saved as well as either you or me; and a soldier is obliged to do as he is bidden. Now Johnny, ye ken, ye war learned to be a doctor o' physic, wad ye no rather try to stop the bleeding and save the young officer's life, as either kill him or let him bleed to death on our floor, when the blame o' the murder might fa' on us?'

"'Now, the blessing of heaven light on your head, my dear Sally!' said the lover, 'for you have spoken the very sentiments of my heart; and, since it is your desire, though we should both rue it, I here vow to you that I

will not only endeavour to save his life, but I will defend
it against our own party to the last drop of my blood.'

"He then began, and, in spite of my feeble struggles,
who knew not either what I was doing or suffering, sewed
up the hideous gash in my throat and neck, tying every
stitch by itself; and the house not being able to produce
a pair of scissors, it seems that he cut off all the odds
and ends of the stitching with a large sharp gully knife;
and it was likely to have been during the operation that
this gentleman chanced to look in at the window. He
then bathed the wound for an hour with cloths dipped in
cold water, dressed it with plaster of wood-betony, and
put me to bed, expressing to his sweetheart the most
vivid hopes of my recovery.

"These operations were scarcely finished when the
maid's two brothers came home from their hiding-
place; and it seems they would have been there much
sooner had not this gentleman given them chase in the
contrary direction. They, seeing the floor all covered
with blood, inquired the cause with wild trepidation of
manner. Their sister was the first to inform them of
what had happened, on which both the young men
gripped to their weapons, and the eldest, Samuel, cried
out with the vehemence of a maniac,—'Blessed be the
righteous avenger of blood! Hoo! It is then true that
the Lord hath delivered our greatest enemy into our
hands!' 'Hold, hold, dearest brother!' cried the maid,
spreading out her arms before him, 'Would you kill a
helpless young man lying in a state of insensibility?
What, although the Almighty hath put his life in your
hand, will he not require the blood of you, shed in such
a base and cowardly way?'

"'Hold your peace, foolish girl,' cried he, in the same furious strain, 'I tell you if he had a thousand lives I would sacrifice them all this moment! Wo be to this old rusty and fizenless sword that did not sever his head from his body when I had a fair chance in the open field! Nevertheless he shall die; for you do not yet know that he hath, within these few hours, murdered our father, whose blood is yet warm around him on the bleak height.'

"'Oh! merciful heaven! killed our father!' screamed the girl, and flinging herself down on the resting-chair, she fainted away. The two brothers regarded not, but with their bared weapons made towards the closet, intent on my blood, and both vowing I should die if I had a thousand lives. The stranger interfered, and thrust himself into the closet door before them, swearing that, before they committed so cowardly a murder, they should first make their way through his body.

"Samuel retreated one step to have full sway of his weapon, and the fury depicted on his countenance proved his determination. But in a moment his gallant opponent closed with him, and holding up his wrist with his left hand, he with the right bestowed on him a blow with such energy that he fell flat on the floor among the soldier's blood. The youngest then ran on their antagonist with his sword and wounded him, but the next moment he was lying beside his brother. As soon as her brothers came fairly to their senses, the young woman and her lover began and expostulated with them, at great length, on the impropriety and unmanliness of the attempt, until they became all of one mind, and the two brothers agreed to join in the defence of the wounded gentleman, from all of their own party, until he was rescued by his friends, which they did. But it was the maid's simple eloquence that finally prevailed with the fierce Covenanters.

"When my brothers came at last, with a number of my men, and took me away, the only thing I remember seeing in the house was the corpse of the old man whom I had shot, and the beautiful girl standing weeping over the body; and certainly my heart smote me in such a manner that I would not experience the same feeling again for the highest of this world's benefits. That comely young maiden and her brave intrepid lover, it would be the utmost ingratitude in me, or in any of my family, ever to forget; for it is scarcely possible that a man can ever be again in the same circumstances as I was, having been preserved from death in the house of the man whom my hand had just deprived of life."

Just as he ended, the sick nurse peeped in, which she had done several times before, and said,—"Will your honour soon be disengaged, d'ye think? for ye see because there's a lass wanting till speak till ye."

"A lass, nurse? what lass can have any business with me? what is she like?"

"Oo 'deed, sir, the lass is weel enough for that part o't, but she may be nae better than she should be for a' that; ye ken, I's no answer for that, for ye see because *like* is an ill mark; but she has been aften up, speering after ye, an' gude troth she's fairly in nettle-earnest now, for she winna gang awa till she see your honour."

The nurse being desired to show her in, a comely girl entered, with a timid step, and seemed ready to faint with trepidation. She had a mantle on, and a hood that

covered much of her face. The privy councillor spoke
to her, desiring her to come forward, and say her errand,
on which she said that "she only wanted a preevat word
wi' the captain, if he was that weel as to speak to ane."
He looked over the bed, and desired her to say on, for
that gentleman was his brother, from whom he kept no
secrets. After a hard struggle with her diffidence, but,
on the other hand, prompted by the urgency of the case,
she at last got out,—" I 'm unco glad to see you sae weel
comed round again, though I daresay ye'll maybe no ken
wha I am. But it was me that nursed ye, an' took care
o' ye in our house, when your head was amaist cuttit
off."

There was not another word required to draw forth
the most ardent expressions of kindness from the two
brothers, on which the poor girl took courage, and, after
several showers of tears, she said, with many bitter sobs,
—"There's a poor lad wha, in my humble opinion,
saved your life; an' wha is just gaun to be hanged
the day after the morn. I would unco fain beg your
honour's interest to get his life spared."

" Say not another word, my dear, good girl," said the
councillor, "for though I hardly know how I can intercede
for a rebel who has taken up arms against the government, yet for your sake, and his, my best interest shall
be exerted."

" Oh, ye maun just say, sir, that the poor Whigs were
driven to desperation, and that this young man was
misled by others in the fervour and enthusiasm of youth.
What else can ye say? but ye're good! oh, ye're very
good! and on my knees I beg that ye winna lose any
time, for indeed there is nae time to lose!"

The councillor lifted her kindly by both hands, and desired her to stay with his brother's nurse till his return, on which he went away to the president, and in half-an-hour returned with a respite for the convict, John Lindsay, for three days, which he gave to the girl, along with an order for her admittance to the prisoner. She thanked him with the tears in her eyes, but added, " Oh, sir, will he and I then be obliged to part forever at the end of three days?"

" Keep up your heart, and encourage your lover," said he, " and meet me here again on Thursday, at this same hour, for, till the council meet, nothing further than this can be obtained."

It may well be conceived how much the poor forlorn prisoner was astonished when his own beloved Sally entered to him with the reprieve in her hand, and how much his whole soul dilated when, on the Thursday following, she presented him with a free pardon. They were afterwards married, when the Gilmours took them under their protection. Lindsay became a highly qualified surgeon, and the descendants of this intrepid youth occupy respectable situations in Edinburgh to this present day.

THE CAMERONIAN'S DREAM.

BY JAMES HISLOP.

In a dream of the night I was wafted away,
To the muirland of mist where the martyrs lay;
Where Cameron's sword and his Bible are seen,
Engraved on the stone where the heather grows green.

'Twas a dream of those ages of darkness and blood,
When the minister's home was the mountain and wood;
When in Wellwood's dark valley the standard of Zion,
All bloody and torn 'mong the heather was lying.

'Twas morning; and summer's young sun from the east
Lay in loving repose on the green mountain's breast;
On Wardlaw and Cairntable the clear shining dew
Hung bright on the heath-bells and mountain-flowers blue.

And far up in heaven, near the white sunny cloud,
The song of the lark was melodious and loud,
And in Glenmuir's wild solitude, lengthened and deep,
Were the whistling of plovers and bleating of sheep.

And Wellwood's sweet valleys breathed music and gladness,
The fresh meadow blooms hung in beauty and redness;
Its daughters were happy to hail the returning,
And drink the enjoyments of July's sweet morning.

But, oh! there were hearts cherished far other feelings,
Illumed by the light of prophetic revealings,
Who drank from the scenery of beauty but sorrow,
For they knew that their blood would bedew it to-morrow.

'Twas the few faithful ones who with Cameron were lying,
Concealed 'mong the mist where the heathfowl was crying,
For the horsemen of Earlshall around them were hovering,
And their bridle reins rung through the thin misty covering.

Their faces grew pale, and their swords were unsheathed,
But the vengeance that darkened their brow was unbreathed;
With eyes turned to heaven in calm resignation,
They sung their last song to the God of Salvation.

The hills with the deep mournful music were ringing,
The curlew and plover in concert were singing;
But the melody died 'mid derision and laughter,
As the host of ungodly rushed on to the slaughter.

Though in mist and in darkness and fire they were shrouded,
Yet the souls of the righteous were calm and unclouded,
Their dark eyes flashed lightning, as, firm and unbending,
They stood like the rock which the thunder is rending.

The muskets were flashing, the blue swords were gleaming,
The helmets were cleft, and the red blood was streaming,
The heavens grew dark and the thunder was rolling,
When in Wellwood's dark muirland the mighty were falling.

When the righteous had fallen, and the combat was ended,
A chariot of fire through the dark cloud descended;
Its drivers were angels on horses of whiteness,
And its burning wheels turned on axles of brightness.

A seraph unfolded its doors bright and shining,
All dazzling like gold of the seventh refining,
And the souls that came forth out of great tribulation,
Have mounted the chariots and steeds of salvation.

On the arch of the rainbow the chariot is gliding,
Through the path of the thunder the horsemen are riding;
Glide swiftly, bright spirits! the prize is before ye,
A crown never fading, a kingdom of glory!

NEW YEAR IN SCOTLAND.

By Edmund S. Roscoe.

From time immemorial, New Year's Eve has been celebrated in Scotland under the name of " Hogmanay." Notwithstanding the labours of our ablest antiquarian etymologists, the derivation of this term still remains a *quæstio vexata.* Plausible speculations have been offered, all of which, however, are inconclusive, although respectively supported with great show of erudition. It is argued that the word is traceable to " Hogmonat," the Icelandic name of Christmas Day, signifying the time of slaughter for sacrifices; and undoubtedly certain familiar Scottish customs of the time seem to have originated amongst the fierce worshippers of Thor and Odin. Again, it has been attempted to identify Hogmanay with one of the four annual festivals of the Druids, which was held on the eve of the 10th of March, the New Year's Day of their reckoning, when they cut down the mistletoe, or " heal-all," from the oak with golden knives or sickles, receiving it reverently in a white linen cloth. Another theory professes to derive Hogmanay from the French. The ancient alliance between France and Scotland introduced a variety of French words into the Scottish language, most of which still survive in the " broad Scotch." According to this view, which has a good deal of probability to recommend it, the term Hogmanay becomes resolvable into a simple corruption of the old French cry at Christmas, " *Au gui menez!*" (To the mistletoe go!) And, indeed, the well-known Scots refrain,

> " Hogmanay,
> Trollolay!
> Give us of your white bread, and none of your gray!"

seems partly a corruption, partly a literal translation, of what was " said or sung" by the Christmas mummers in France: " *Au gui menez! Tire-lire! Maint du blanc, et point du bas!*" Finally, Hogmanay inaugurates what the Scottish people call " the daft days," corresponding to the French *fete de fous.* So much for the etymology of the thing. We leave the knotty point to the plodding tribe of Dryasdusts, in whose labyrinthine province it lies. Our business just now is to record homely reminiscences of the reddest-letter days in the popular Scottish calendar.

Some curious observances connected with the New Year season—perhaps vestiges of the ancient Celtic heathenism—have lingered long in the Highlands, though now modified by the spread of intelligence. Hogmanay is unknown to the Gaelic; the term " Nolliag," in that language, being applied both to Christmas and the New Year. During last century the old fashions were in full sway. All work was ostentatiously laid aside on the afternoon of the 31st December, and the men of a *clachan* or hamlet repaired to the wood, and cut down a number of juniper-bushes, which they carried home on their backs in preparation for the strange ceremonial of the morrow. Each household also procured a pitcher of water from " the dead and living ford "—that is, the ford in a river by which funerals and passengers crossed. This water was brought in perfect silence, and without the vessel being allowed to touch the ground in its progress, as contact with the earth would have destroyed the virtue of the spell involved. At an early hour next morning every dwelling was the scene of singular rites, which were supposed to preserve against witchcraft, the evil eye, and other " devilments," during the year then begun. The father, or head of the house, was the first to rise. He kindled the fire, and then, taking the charmed water and a brush, treated the rest of the family, old and young, who were still a-bed, to a profuse aspersion, which was generally acknowledged with any thing but gratitude. What remained of the water was still farther enchanted by being poured over an oval-shaped crystal, or a long-hoarded piece of silver money, and then carried to the byre (which, in most cases, was under the same roof with the cottage), where it was given to the bestial to drink. On returning, the operator heaped part of the juniper-bushes on the hearth, and carefully closing and stuffing the doors, windows, and every *bole* or crevice which could admit the slightest breath of air, set fire to the pile. The dense smoke thence arising speedily reduced the inmates to the point of suffocation. When the fresh air was re-admitted, a stout glass of whisky, which "had never seen the gauger," was served round; and the cattle were next subjected to similar fumigation, which concluded the painful solemnities of the morning. At the present day, it is only in remote districts that such "cantrips" continue to be practised, and even there the bestial alone are favoured with the charmed water and the juniper smoke. It will be recollected that the Mussulmans of India use lamp and smoke charms for casting out devils and curing diseases. But belief in the influence of the evil eye on cows and horses is still prevalent in the Highlands, although, happily, the antidote to this malignant power is well known. The owner of the threatened animal, if it be a cow, has nothing more to do than to offer the suspected person a little of its milk; or, if it be a horse, to name a price, however extravagant, at which he is willing to sell it.

A farcical Hogmanay prank in Coll, one of the Hebrides, had the honour of being noticed by Doctor Johnson, in his *Journey to the Western Islands:* "At New Year's Eve, in the hall or castle of the laird, where,

at festal seasons, there may be supposed a very numerous
company, one man dresses himself in a cow's hide, upon
which other men beat with sticks. He runs with all
this noise round the house, which all the company quit
in a counterfeited fright. The door is then shut. At
New Year's Eve there is no great pleasure to be had out
of doors in the Hebrides. They are sure soon to recover
from their terror enough to solicit readmission; which,
for the honour of poetry, is not to be obtained but by
repeating a verse, with which those that are knowing and
provident take care to be furnished."

Other Highland usages of the season, common in our
time, assimilate to those of the lowlands. Young people
stroll about on Hogmanay, chanting appropriate rhymes;
whilst their seniors amuse themselves, over brimming
bumpers of "mountain-dew," with Ossianic or Bardic
songs, and *sguelachd*, or fabulous stories, of a class more
wonderful than the *Arabian Nights*. Next day numerous
parties from the clachans contend at the *Camanachd*
(shinty, or club-ball), an ancient and favourite pastime,
better adapted than even "Scotland's ain game o'
curling" for a cold winter day in the north.

The Highlanders pay special regard to the direction
of the wind on New Year's night, believing that it fore-
shows the weather that shall characterize the year. Thus,
north wind portends cold and storms; east wind, abundance of fruit on the trees; south wind, heat and plenty;
west wind, abundance of fish and milk. They prefer
that the first three days of winter should be gloomy,
which they reckon as the sign of a good year. Prognos-
tications of the weather for each month are also drawn
from that of the twelve days beginning with 31st

December. Thus, Hogmanay prefigures the month of January; New Year's Day, February; 2nd January, March; and so on.

Throughout the Lowlands, the sedate and canny Scots keep New Year-tide with a degree of merry-making that partakes of saturnalian jollity; the "mirth and fun" extending over "the daft days," or interval from Hogmanay to Handsel-Monday, the first Monday after New Year. The purists of the Kirk were never able to suppress Hogmanay, evidently because they could not associate it with Popery. A Covenanting divine is reported to have stigmatized it in a sermon by the following *outre* definition:—"Sirs, do you know what Hogmanay signifies? It is—the devil be in the house; that's the meaning of the Hebrew original." But his hearers were not to be frightened by etymological terrors; and from his time to ours, Hogmanay and "the daft days" have kept their place. As the poet of "The Sabbath" says:—

> " Of all the festive nights which customs old
> And waning fast have made the poor man's own,
> The merriest of them all is Hogmanay.
> Then from each cottage window, 'mid the gloom,
> A brighter ray shoots through the falling flakes,
> And glimmering lanterns gleam, like will-o'-wisp,
> Athwart the fields, or, mounting over stiles
> Evanish suddenly.   No dread is now
> Of walking wraith, or witch, or cantrip fell:
> For superstition's self this night assumes
> A smiling aspect and a fearless mien,
> And tardy prudence slips the leash from joy."

Early on the last evening of the year bands of boys go from house to house, in town and country, " singing for carls," as it is called—these " carls," being oaten three-cornered cakes, baked for the occasion, and distributed along with slices of cheese. But much of the old picturesqueness of the custom has died out. In Scotland, masking at Hogmanay is termed " guizing," and maskers are " guizards." The glory of the " guizards" has departed. Arrayed in such fantastic habiliments as they could muster, and wearing pasteboard " fause faces," they enacted a sort of rhymical drama, closely resembling that known in England as " St. George's Play." The *dramatis personæ* comprised Galatian, or Galatius (probably the Caledonian king, Galgacus, who fought Agricola at the battle of the Grampians), the Black Knight, Dr. Brown (who cured dead men), Devil Doubt, or Judas (who bore the traditional bag), and Bessie, the Talking Man or Chorus. This tragi-comedy has almost entirely fallen into oblivion, doubtless from the trouble of committing it to memory. The singing-boys, who represent the guizards, still affect disguise by blackening their faces with soot, or putting on the pasteboard masks with which the toy-shop windows are hideous for weeks before Hogmanay; but their performance is limited to a popular song, prefaced by the following rhymes:—

> " Get up, gudewife, and dinna be sweir
> To deal your bread as lang 's you 're here;
> The day will come when you 'll be dead,
> And neither want ale nor bread.
> Get up, gudewife, and shak' your feathers,
> And dinna think that we are beggars;
> For we 're bonny bairns come out to play:
> Get up, and gie 's our Hogmanay."

And, accordingly, they get their Hogmanay, in the shape of " carls " or halfpence.

The guizing and guizards of old times could not fail to provoke the ire of the kirk, and high censures were from time to time pronounced, but all to little purpose. Such denunciations were equally ineffectual when directed against what was considered an analogous form of masking. In the seventeenth century and later, the Scottish women of all degrees were fond of wearing a light plaid or "tartan screen," disposed about the head and shoulders in such a way as that it could be used as a veil to conceal the face in public, "at kirk or market." This fashion was pertinaciously condemned from all the pulpits, and the ecclesiastical mind waxed so bitter that the Kirk Session of Monifeith (a Forfarshire parish) passed an order, on the 17th September, 1643, directing their beddal, or officer, "to buy ane pynt of tar to put upon the women that hold the plaid about their head in the church"—that is to say, the fair delinquents were to be tarred like so many sheep. Nevertheless, the plaid-veil survived to Allan Ramsay's day, as testified by one of his finest lyrics:—

> " Now wat ye wha I met yestreen
>   Coming down the street, my joe?
> My mistress, in her tartan screen,
>   Fu' bonnie, braw, and sweet, my joe."

But to return to Hogmanay. Long before midnight the singing-boys have disappeared with their wallets of " carls;" and as the witching time approaches, the streets of a town gradually become crowded with lads of the artizan class, waiting to usher in the coming year, the chief place of rendezvous being the market-cross. Nobody can think of retiring to rest till after " that hour o' night's black arch the keystane." At last the clock strikes twelve, and each stroke is welcomed by the eager assemblage at the cross with a cheer that might rouse the dead. Numbers now rush away, at headlong speed, on first-footing expeditions, leaving the rest shaking hands, wishing "a gude New Year and a merry Handsel-Monday," and filling-up and tossing off bumpers. Meanwhile the street wells are environed by giggling damsels with pitchers and pans, each striving to obtain "the cream o' the well"—that is, the first draught of water after twelve o'clock, which insures good-luck throughout the year, coupled with the certainty of a husband. About forty or fifty years ago, the "hot pint" was all the rage on New Year's morning. It was compounded of warm ale, whisky, and sugar—a most heady mixture—which was carried about in copper kettles, and dispensed in the streets, as well as in every household favoured by the visit of a first-foot. But the kettle with its hot pint has long been superseded by the everlasting whisky-bottle.

First-footing is still in high favour amongst the mass of the population, great faith being placed in the good or bad luck attending a first-foot or individual who first enters a house on New Year's morning; and it so happens that the man or woman enjoying the reputation of being lucky is specially solicited to act as first-foot to several families, who keep their doors fast locked till the expected visitor arrives. The first-foot must not enter a house empty-handed, and therefore brings bread and cheese, in addition to the indispensable bottle. "The folk will be visiting you with their bottles on New Year's morning," said a clerical friend to old George Cooper, the present centenarian of Caithness. "Ay," answered

George, "they only bring bottles to my house; but when they gang to yours, they tak' a nine-gallon cask."

The most extraordinary and inexplicable Hogmanay custom in Scotland is that called "burning the clavie," which annually enlivens the fishing-village of Burghead, on the Moray Firth. Its origin and import have hitherto baffled the researches of the learned. The "clavie" consists chiefly of a tar-barrel, which, being ignited in the gloaming, is carried about the town in triumph, and then deposited on the top of a neighbouring eminence, from which, however, it is speedily displaced, and rolled down to the bottom. The unmeaning ceremony is concluded by the crowd knocking the blazing "clavie" to pieces. Formerly the "clavie" was carried along the shore, where vessels were lying; but this part of the programme, so apt to lead to dangerous consequences, is now wisely omitted.

On New Year's Day the most of people will neither borrow, lend, nor give anything whatever out of their houses, for fear of their luck suffering. Even so trivial a matter as a light is refused, and angrily refused, too. The floor must not be swept, for the same reason; and it is a bad sign if the fire goes out, as that portends death. All over Scotland the day is celebrated with unrestrained festivity. A superstitious anxiety is expressed to enter on the New Year with "routh o' roughness," or plenty to eat and drink, the contrary being an evil omen. The very poorest do their best to provide "something bye ordinar'" to hold good cheer, and, to all appearance, they attain their object, if streets filled with drunken people from morning till night can form a criterion. Even the paupers in our poor-houses are treated to a

New Year's supper, which is graced by the presence of the leading managers.

In England, as far back as the reign of Henry VI., it was usual to present gifts to the monarch on New Year's Day morning. The same custom prevailed at the Scottish Court, as shown by the existing accounts ot the Lord High Treasurer. Thus, on 1st January, 1490, ten angels, value twelve pounds, were "given to the king (James IV.) in his bed, in the morning." Nor was the custom one-sided. " Giff gaff maks gude friends," quoth the proverb. The king gave as well as got. On 1st January, 1507, a largesse was granted, by the royal command, to a party of minstrels numbering sixty-nine persons. On 1st January, 1526, King James V. spent twenty pounds " yat nycht, eftir supper, in mummyn," and distributed rings in presents to the value of thirty pounds. In subsequent years, during the same reign, " play-coats " for maskers were provided, and also gold chains, rings, tablets, " and other golden work," to be given in New Year's gifts. But if a custom of making gifts on New Year's-Day was ever general among the people, it has long been transferred, in the central counties of Scotland, to Handsel-Monday, the word *handsel* in this connection signifying gift. Till of late years, Handsel-Monday was reckoned by the old style. At no distant period it was " the principal day with the working-classes " of a town, says a local historian. " By one in the morning, the streets were in an uproar with young people, who appeared to consider themselves privileged to do whatever mischief they pleased. It was a constant practice to pull down signboards, or anything that came in their way, and make a large bonfire with them at the cross. . . The tradesmen were all idle this day, and considered themselves entitled to *handsel* from their employers, and even from individuals in any way connected with the business. Thus, the weavers having received their handsel from the manufacturer, a deputation from the shop was sent to the wright who made their utensils, another to the reedmaker and to the chandler who supplied them with candles, and a third to the company who boiled the yarn. The whole proceeds of these begging commissions were put together, and spent in the evening at a tavern." Handsel-Monday is still a jovial holiday, the universal feeling being that, at this tide, " dancing, and drinking, and singing's nae crime." The youngsters expect their handsel in the morning, and it is bestowed ungrudgingly. There is a total cessation of labour and business. The mechanic, shopman, ploughman, all are free. But this holiday is the one peculiarly entwined with the domestic habits and affections of the peasantry. The sons and daughters of a humble household, who have left the paternal roof, make a point of spending Handsel-Monday, if possible, with " the auld folk at hame" and so there is many a happy reunion around cottage firesides. The old style has now been abandoned, which is a wise reform; for, though boisterous excess has in a large measure become obsolete, the use of " Scotland's scaith " at this season is too liberal; and the new arrangement, by which the " daft days " are considerably reduced in number, cannot but ultimately be productive of the best results. And now, having discoursed so fully on the New Year customs of Scotland, we take farewell of the reader, with the hearty wish of a national poet:—

" A happy New Year, a happy New Year!
To the friend and the foe, to the far and the near;
Here's wishing them health, meikle wisdom, and wealth,
And mony a merry and happy New Year !"

From " Belgravia."

ON SEEING A CAT AND A KITTEN ASLEEP IN THE BED WHERE BURNS WAS BORN.

By the Rev. P. Hately Waddell, LL.D.

Immortal, truthful, tender shade,
Friendly to all that God hath made—
    No hate, no scorn—
Look with a smile on the strange pair
That shelter in the sacred air
    Where thou wast born.

Asleep, or feigning, *a la mort*,
Malice, and treachery, and sport,
    Superbly furred;
The living opposites of thee—
A tigress and her progeny,
    In one plain word.

Yet why not here—where thousands look?
In this the self-same, holy nook,
    Profound and low,
Where truth and pity, manly worth,
With music added at their birth,
    Began to glow.

Puss, puss, thou hast a moral here—
God grant us sense to read it clear,
    And profit by it.

Mother and daughter, coiled in one,
Craft, falsehood, cruelty, and fun,
 Disarmed and quiet.

Oh, power of love, supreme thou art
In this, God's cradle of the heart,
 And bed of song.
Who visits here, with soul unmoved,
With fraud unchecked, greed unreproved,
 Still choosing wrong:

Who sees not better God's great plan,
Who loves not better beast and man,
 Let him withdraw.
Here God doth teach humility,
Here God enjoins all charity,
 Here love is law.

     Contributed.

THE LEGEND OF SAINT SWITHIN.

A DEESIDE BALLAD. BY GEORGE DAVIDSON.

SAINT SWITHIN was a drouthy saint—
 When in *retreat* at Blairs,
He drank a pitcher full of grog
 Before his morning prayers.

And duly quaffed throughout the day—
 Whene'er he told his beads;
A pint at every *pater*,
 And a gallon at the *creeds*.

And from morn till night the Sacristan
 Did little else but jog
With pails of water from the Dee,
 To mix St. Swithin's grog.

But July came with sultry sun,
  And clear and cloudless sky,
And parched up all the country round,
  Till every well ran dry.

The mountain springs and tarns ran dry,
  And scorching drought prevailed ;
The Dee dried up—the Corby Linn—
  The Burn of Culter failed.

And St. Swithin lay perspiring,
  And panting like a dog;
Yet bravely strove to count his beads,
  And loudly called for grog.

And the poor bewildered Sacristan
  Sought fountain, glen, and bog
In vain, for cold spring water,
  To mix St. Swithin's grog.

He sought mill-lades and fountains
  Through all the country round ;
But every pailful was dried up,
  Save in the Abbot's pond :

The churlish Abbot's pond, well stored
  With choice and costly fish—
That served on fasts and festivals
  For many a savoury dish ;

The spacious pond, whose crystal streams,
  Were watched with jealous care,
The poor Sacristan vainly sought
  To fill his pitchers there.

Then home returning weary,
  To St. Swithin he did say—
"I've searched the country far and near,
  This sultry summer's day ;

" And there 's not a drop of water left
    To fill your can or cup;
So your Reverence must give up your glass,
    So long 's the glass keeps up:

" Unless his Grace the Abbot
    Will lend us, in our strait,
A Butt of water from his pond,
    Till next there comes a spate."

"Well counselled good Sacristan! haste,
    And to the Abbot say—
Saint Swithin begs a boon of him,
    And he will ever pray, &c.

" With vigils and with fastings
    His fainting spirits sink;
He 's sought for water everywhere,
    And there 's not a drop to drink:

" And he begs a Butt of water,
    While this sore drought prevails,
A Butt of water from your pond,
    To fill his tubs and pails;

" For one Butt of water daily
    He does most humbly pray;
Which he 'll return with interest
    On the next rainy day."

"St. Swithin!" roared the Abbot,
    " Fie on the drunken rogue!
Dares he propose to drain my pond,
    That he may swig his grog?

" Dares he propose to drain my pond,
    And starve my perch and trout?
Nay! let him take to *Bass's Ale*,
    And *Devanha Double Stout;*

Or, if the knave will drink Schiedam,
   Let him take it *cold without.*"

Such taunting answer to his prayer
   Might well provoke a saint,
And St. Swithin clenched his fist and said—
   "I'll make the churl repent.

"He bids me take to *Bass's Ale,*
   And *Devanha Double Stout,*
Or if I must have Hollands,
   I may take it *cold without.*

"And all, the paltry wretch! to spare
   His perches and his trout!
Just see in four-and-twenty hours
   If I don't serve him out.

"In less than four-and-twenty hours
   I'll show the stingy sinner
Saint Swithin shall enjoy his grog,
   When he shall want his dinner."

Then St. Swithin drained his pitcher,
   And emptied his last can,
And to his lonely cell he went,
   I wot an angry man.

But if he waked, or if he slept,
   No mortal tongue can tell,
I fear he wrought some hellish charm
   Or dreadful magic spell.

For long ere the Sacristan rose
   To ring the matin bell,
The morning sky grew black as night,
   And rain in torrents fell.

Rain torrents poured, and thunder roared,
   And lightnings gleamed o'erhead;

The streams leaped from the mountain side
And swelled the river's bed.

The depths of Ballochbuie's woods,
The furious tempest stirs ;
And down the raging Garawalt
Hurls oaks, and birks, and firs.

One hour the bridge of Ballater
The fearful onset stood ;
Then, quaking, fell with thundering crash
Beneath the foaming flood.

And far through Strahan, the brawling A'an
Swept with tempestuous sough ;
And dark tumultuous waters dashed
Sheer o'er the Brig o' Feugh.

The Corby Linn, with fearsome din,
Rush'd o'er Kingcausie's Brae ;
With headlong turn the Culter Burn
Bore Pirie's Mills away.

Down goes the Abbot's stately tower
Beneath the boiling surge ;
And down the Abbot's spacious pond,
With all his trout and perch.

His bleating flocks, and lowing herds,
A woeful sight to see;
His corn and hay, all swept away
In the wide and wasting Dee.

And still the storm is gathering,
And still the torrents fall ;
When St. Swithin, in his Mackintosh,
Looks o'er the convent wall.

He sternly eyes the mighty stream
That heaves from bank to brae,
And sees the Abbot, 'midst the tide,
Perched on a cole of hay.

Perched on a cole and struggling sore,
He strives to keep afloat,
Still shouting, as he scours along,
" Ho! help—a boat—a boat!!"

Up starts the old Sacristan,
As rose the desperate shout—
" It is his Grace the Abbot's cry,
Haste, haste, and pull him out !"

" Nay," cried St. Swithin, " give the churl
His fill of *cold without*,
And should he reach *Devanha* safe---
Of which I have some doubt—
Let him take a glass of India Ale,
Or a pot of Double Stout."

Then, pointing to his flowing can,
Quoth he " I rather think
'Tis to your Grace's courtesy
We owe our morning's drink."

And raising, with a horrid grin,
The pitcher to his lip—
" I wish your Grace good morning,
And a cool and pleasant trip."

And as the hapless voyager
Was lost amidst the fog—
" So fare it with all churls," said he,
" Who grudge the saints their grog."

July, that fifteenth dismal day,
This fearful spate began,

And forty days and forty nights
Rains fell, and torrents ran.

For forty days and forty nights
The wide and wasting Dee
Rushed o'er her banks and swept her plains,
From Crathie to the sea.

And fertile lands were turned to sands,
And smiling haughs to bog,
And all because St. Swithin vowed,
They should not stop his grog.

And ever since, whene'er a shower
Falls on St. Swithin's day,
'Twill pour for forty days on end—
So ancient ladies say.

By permission of the Author.

THE BRAVE PILOT.

By the Rev. G. T. Hoare.

THE hero of this tale, James Maxwell, was one of a family famous for courage and hardihood. He was a native of Stirlingshire, in Scotland. He and several of his brothers took to a seafaring life, and being intelligent and industrious, rose in time to be masters or pilots of steam-vessels. In the year 1827, James was acting as pilot on board a steamer called the "Clydesdale," which sailed between the Clyde and the west coast of Ireland. One evening, after setting out on the voyage, a smell of fire was perceived on board by Maxwell and the master, both of whom tried hard to discover whence it proceeded;

but in vain. Still it increased, and about eleven o'clock the master sprang on deck, exclaiming hastily, "Maxwell, the flames have burst out at the paddle-box!" James asked quietly in what direction he should steer the vessel, and with one earnest prayer for strength, and for his family at home, he turned all his attention to his work. At first fearing they might be driven on the rocky coast of Galloway, the master was anxious to press forward; but with nothing but the wide ocean before them, this soon appeared such a hopeless course that he resolved to put the steamer towards shore at all risk. Notwithstanding the active efforts of the men, the fire increased, till it was raging furiously. All the passengers rushed to the fore-part of the vessel—the safest place, as the flames were swept by the wind back towards the stern.

There the brave pilot stood, his eyes fixed on the spot he meant to reach, firmly resolved in his heart to keep at his post through all. Had he left the wheel, the ship would have drifted helplessly about, at the mercy of the wind and waves, and the flames would soon have spread to all parts of the ship. By keeping her going the flames were driven in one direction; and if they could only reach the land they might be saved. The master and some of the sailors did all they could to throw water on the spot where Maxwell stood, but soon the fire seized the cabin below him, heating his standing-place to a burning glow. He was shut off from the number assembled on the other end by a roaring mass of smoke and flame. Now and then the wind swept this aside, and they caught sight of him for a moment, keeping his awful watch. The people on shore saw the blazing ship coming fast towards them in the darkness of the night, and by waving lights they tried to point out to those on board the best place for landing.

Now the fire grew hotter and spread further. Maxwell's feet were almost roasted, yet still he kept his post. In another moment he ran the vessel into an opening among the rocks, and alongside a ledge, on which all the crew and passengers escaped safe to shore. The pilot's noble work was done. Even at that instant he could listen to the voice of distress. A man who had reached the shore exclaimed that without his trunk he should be ruined, and offered five pounds to any one who would save it. Maxwell seized the burning trunk and threw it on shore, but so hot was the handle, that his skin actually stuck to it. Then he left the ship himself. It seems almost impossible to believe that the man for whom he had done this forgot to pay the promised reward; but so it was; and James was not likely to ask for it. He never recovered this awful burning. Not only his feet had suffered greatly, but his hair; and his great-coat and cap were in such a state from the heat to which he had been exposed, that they crumbled into powder at a touch. During that dreadful night, his face came to look ten years older, his handsome features were wasted, and what hair remained on his head was changed. All these signs showed plainly how intense and agonizing was the trial he had passed through: and bravely, indeed, had he done his part. After a time he was able, though much weakened by his past sufferings, once more to take up his occupation of pilot. At different times in his life sums of money were raised among those who had heard his story, to enable him to bring up his family. In the year 1840 he died.

GLENARA.

BY THOMAS CAMPBELL.

O HEARD ye yon pibroch sound sad in the gale,
Where a band cometh slowly with weeping and wail?
'Tis the chief of Glenara laments for his dear;
And her sire, and her people, are call'd to her bier.

Glenara came first with the mourners and shroud;
Her kinsmen they follow'd, but mourn'd not aloud:
Their plaids all their bosoms were folded around:
They march'd all in silence,—they look'd on the ground.

In silence they reach'd, over mountain and moor,
To a heath where the oak-tree grew lonely and hoar:
" Now here let us place the grey stone of her cairn:
Why speak ye no word?"—said Glenara the stern.

" And tell me, I charge you! ye clan of my spouse,
Why fold ye your mantles, why cloud ye your brows?"
So spake the rude chieftain :—no answer is made,
But each mantle unfolding, a dagger display'd.

" I dreamt of my lady, I dreamt of her shroud,"
Cried a voice from the kinsmen, all wrathful and loud;
" And empty that shroud and that coffin did seem ;
Glenara! Glenara! now read me my dream! "

Oh! pale grew the cheek of that chieftain, I ween,
When the shroud was unclos'd, and no lady was seen;
When a voice from the kinsmen spoke louder in scorn,
'Twas the youth who had lov'd the fair Ellen of Lorn :

" I dreamt of my lady, I dreamt of her grief,
I dreamt that her lord was a barbarous chief:

I

On a rock of the ocean fair Ellen did seem;
Glenara! Glenara! now read me my dream!"

In dust low the traitor has knelt to the ground,
And the desert reveal'd where his lady was found;
From a rock of the ocean that beauty is borne—
Now joy to the house of fair Ellen of Lorn!

ROB ROY'S DEFENCE OF HIMSELF TO MR. OSBALDISTONE.

BY SIR WALTER SCOTT.

You speak like a boy—like a boy, who thinks the old gnarled oak can be twisted as easily as the young sapling. Can I forget that I have been branded as an outlaw, stigmatized as a traitor, a price set on my head as if I had been a wolf, my family treated as the dam and cubs of a hill-fox, whom all may torment, vilify, degrade, and insult; the very name which came to me from a long and noble line of martial ancestors, denounced, as if it were a spell to conjure up the devil with?

And they *shall* find that the name they have dared to proscribe—that the name of MacGregor *is* a spell to raise the wild devil withal. *They* shall hear of my vengeance, that would scorn to listen to the story of my wrongs. The miserable Highland drover, bankrupt, barefooted, stripped of all, dishonoured and hunted down, because the avarice of others grasped at more than that poor all could pay, shall burst on them in an awful change. They that scoffed at the grovelling worm, and trod upon him, may cry and howl when they see the

stoop of the flying and fiery-mouthed dragon. But why
do I speak of all this?—only ye may opine it frets my
patience to be hunted like an otter, or a seal, as a salmon
upon the shallows, and that by my very friends and
neighbours; and to have as many sword-cuts made, and
pistols flashed at me, as I had this day in the ford of
Avondow, would try a saint's temper, much more a
Highlander's, who are not famous for that good gift, as
you may have heard. But one thing bides me of what
Nicoll said. I'm vexed when I think of Robert and
Hamish living their father's life. But let us say no more
of this. . . .

You must think hardly of us, and it is not natural that
it should be otherwise. But remember, at least, we have
not been unprovoked:—we are a rude and an ignorant,
and it may be, a violent and passionate, but we are not a
cruel people. The land might be at peace and in law
for us, did they allow us to enjoy the blessings of peaceful
law. But we have been a persecuted people; and if
persecution maketh wise men mad, what must it do to
men like us, living as our fathers did a thousand years
since, and possessing scarce more lights than they did?
Can we view their bloody edicts against us—their hang-
ing, heading, hounding, and hunting down an ancient
and honourable name—as deserving better treatment
than that which enemies give to enemies? Here I stand
—have been in twenty frays, and never hurt man but
when I was in hot blood!—and yet they would betray me,
and hang me like a masterless dog, at the gate of any
great man that has an ill-will at me.

You are a kind hearted and an honourable youth, and
understand, doubtless, that which is due to the feelings

of a man of honour. But the heather that I have trod upon when living must bloom over me when I am dead —my heart would sink, and my arm would shrink and wither, like fern in the frost, were I to lose sight of my native hills; nor has the world a scene that would console me for the loss of the rocks and cairns, wild as they are, that you see around us. And Helen—what would become of her, were I to leave her, the subject of new insult and atrocity?—or how could she bear to be removed from these scenes, where the remembrance of her wrong is aye sweetened by the recollection of her revenge? I was once so hard put at by my great enemy, as I may well call him, that I was forced e'en to give way to the tide, and removed myself, and my people, and my family, from our dwellings in our native land, and to withdraw for a time into MacCallummore's country,—and Helen made a lament on our departure, as well as MacRimmon himself could have framed it; and so piteously sad and woesome, that our hearts almost brake as we listened to her;—it was like the wailing of one for the mother that bore him—and I would not have the same touch of the heart-break again, . . . no, not to have all the lands that were ever owned by MacGregor.

BAGPIPES *versus* FIDDLE.

BY WILLIAM ANDERSON.

I' THE haugh where the Don rins by bonny Braidha',
In a cot i' the clachan dwelt Murdo Macraw,

Weel kent far and near as a frolicksome blade—
A piper for sport, and a thatcher for trade.

There wasna a cliack, a dancin', or fair,
A weddin', or christ'nin', but Murdo was there;
Wi' his pipes an' his drones he wad baith skirl an' blaw—
An' muckle requested was Murdo Macraw.

To neighbourin' farmers in hairst he wad shear—
He could trap hares and rabbits, or sawmon could spear;
Brak' dogs for the huntin' o' otters an' brocks,
Or fettle at guns, either barrels or locks.

He made rods for fishin', an' twistit their lines—
The lasses lo'ed Murdo, and he lo'ed the queans;
Nae ane in particular, he courtit them a'—
They were whiles like to fecht about Murdo Macraw.

An affair that occurr'd gied his credit a shog;
To Braidha' cam' a wricht a' the way frae Drumclog—
A canty wee chiel', wha could handle the bow,
At the new country dances, like Donald or Gow.

Country dances were now a' the rage o' the day,
An' Murdo could play but a reel or strathspey;
Sae seldom, if ever, he now got a ca'—
'Tis a cursed piece o' business, thocht Murdo Macraw.

The hairst was ta'en in, and the rucks got a hap—
The fodder was lang, an' a bountiful crap;
I' the gloamin' the grieve stappit o'er to the wricht,
As the cliack was to be on the Wednesday nicht.

But after the lads an' the lasses were met,
Ye needna misdoot that they a' lookit blate,
For somehow the wricht through the day gaed awa—
They had nae ither help but seek Murdo Macraw.

Macraw thocht a slur on his pipes had been cast,
He demurr'd for a while, but consentit at last;
The pipes were ta'en down, an' he dress'd himsel' braw—
Ye may judge sic a welcome he got at Braidha'.

He scarcely had played twa strathspeys to the ear,
When the canty wee fiddler cam' in wi' a steer;
The fiddle was straikit wi' mony a " ha, ha!"
An' few tint a thocht upon Murdo Macraw.

The supper was ower, an' the lasses were fain
To be on the floor at the dancin' again;
But ye ken disappointments are ilka ane's lot—
The fiddle was lost, an' it couldna be got.

They lookit the " but," and ransackit the " ben,"
But nae ane could guess whare the fiddle was gane.
Then they cried for the pipes—they were also awa;
" They are after the fiddle," said Murdo Macraw.

Says Forbes, the grieve, " 'Tis remarkable queer
How bagpipes an' fiddle should baith disappear;
First married who gets them "—when, strange-like to tell,
They were found 'neath the barm in a tubfu' o' ale.

They drew out the fiddle, completely a wrack,
The wricht lookit gloomy, tho' naething he spak';
Nae waur were the pipes, wi' a squeeze an' a blaw—
" Tak' ye that for your fiddling," thocht Murdo Macraw.

_____

JOHN BROWN OF PRIESTHILL.

By the Rev. George Gilfillan.

IN 1684, the common soldiers were empowered, without indictment or trial, to put to death suspicious persons,

if they refused to take the oaths, or to answer the
questions which they pressed upon them.   Hence
occurred the never-to-be-forgotten murder of John
Brown, the Ayrshire carrier.   This man lived at a
house (still standing, we believe) called Priesthill, in
the parish of Muirkirk.   It occupied an eminence com-
manding a wide and waste view of heath, mosses, and
rocks.   John Brown was an amiable and blameless man.
He had taken no part in the risings or public testifyings
of the times.   His only crimes were, his non-attendance
on the curate of the parish, and his occasionally retiring,
with some like-minded, to a favourite ravine among the
moors, where they spent the Sabbath-day in praise and
prayer.   His wife was a noble spirit: blythe, leal-hearted,
humorous even.   He, on the other hand, was gravely
mild and sedate, and her smile shone on him like
sunshine on a dunhill-side, and transfigured him into
gladness.   His family was one of peace, although Isabel
Weir was his second wife, and there were children of
the first alive.   All were wont to pour out, like blood
from one heart, to meet him, when he was seen approaching on his pack-horse from his distant excursions.
Latterly, as the persecution fell darker, and closed in
around those Ayrshire wolds, John could no longer ply
his trade; nay, was even compelled, occasionally, to
leave his home, and spend days and nights in the
remoter solitudes of the country.   Nevertheless, his
hour at last arrived.   It was the 30th of April, 1685.
John Brown had been at home, and unmolested for
some time: he had risen early, and had performed public
worship.   The psalm sung was the twenty-seventh; and
the chapter read the sixteenth of John; which closes

with the remarkable words, " In the world ye shall have
tribulation: but be of good cheer, I have overcome the
world." His prayer was, as usual, powerful and fervent;
for, although he stuttered in common speech, he never
stuttered in prayer: he could not but speak fluently in
the dialect of heaven! He then went away alone to the
hill to prepare some peat-ground. Meanwhile Claverhouse had come in late at night to Lesmahagow, where
a garrison was posted; had heard of John; had risen
still earlier than his victim; and by six on that gray
April morning had tracked him to the moss; had
surrounded him with three troops of dragoons, and led
him down to the door of his own house. With the
dignity of Cincinnatus, leaving his plough in mid-furrow,
John dropped his spade, and walked down, it is said,
"rather like a leader than a captive." His wife was
warned of their approach, and, with more than the
heroism of an ancient Roman matron, with one boy in
her arms, with a girl in her hand, and, alas! *with a child
within her*, Isabel Weir came calmly out to play her
part in this frightful tragedy!

Claverhouse was no trifler. Short and sharp was he
always in his brutal trade. He asked John at once why
he did not attend the curate, and if he would pray for
the king. John stated, in one distinct sentence, the
usual Covenanting reasons. On hearing it, Claverhouse
exclaimed, " Go to your knees, for you shall immediately
die!" John complied, without remonstrance, and proceeded to pray, in terms so melting, and with such
earnest supplication for his wife and their born and
unborn children, that Claverhouse saw the hard eyes of
his dragoons beginning to moisten, and their hands to

tremble, and thrice interrupted him with volleys of blasphemy. When the prayer was ended, John turned round to his wife, reminded her that this was the day come of which he had told her when he first proposed marriage to her, and asked her if she was willing to part with him. "Heartily willing," was her reply. "This," he said, "is all I desire. I have nothing more now to do but to die." He then kissed her and the children, and said, "May all purchased and promised blessings be multiplied unto you!" "No more of this," roared out the savage, whose own iron heart this scene was threatening to move. "You six dragoons, there, fire on the fanatic!" They stood motionless, the prayer had quelled them. Fearing a mutiny, both among his soldiers and in his own breast, he snatched a pistol from his belt and shot the good man through the head. He fell, his brains spurted out, and his brave wife caught the shattered head in her lap. "What do you think of your husband now?" howled the ruffian. "I aye thocht muckle o' him, sir, but never sae muckle as I do this day." "I would think little to lay thee beside him," he answered. "If you were permitted, I doubt not you would; but how are ye to answer for this morning's work?" "To men, I can be answerable; and as for God I will take Him in my own hands!" And, with these desperate words, he struck spurs to his horse, and led his dragoons away from the inglorious field. Meekly and calmly did this heroic and Christian woman tie up her husband's head in a napkin, compose his body, cover it with her plaid—and not till these duties were discharged did she permit the pent-up current of her mighty grief to burst out, as she sat down beside the corpse and wept bitterly.

THE YERL O' WATERYDECK.

By George MacDonald, M.A., LL.D.

THE wind it blew, and the ship it flew,
    And it was "Hey for hame!"
But up and cried the skipper to his crew,
    "Haud her oot ower the saut sea faem."

Syne up and spak' the angry king—
    "Haud on for Dumferiine!"
Quo' the skipper, "My lord, this maunna be—
    I'm king o' this boat o' mine."

He tuik the helm intil his han',
    He left the shore un'er the lee;
Syne croodit sail, an' east and south,
    Stude awa richt oot to sea.

Quo' the king, "There 's·treason i' this, I vow;
    This is something un'erhan'!
'Bout ship!" Quo' the skipper, "Yer grace forgets
    Ye are king but o' the lan!"

Oot he held to the open sea,
    Quhile the north wind flaughtered and fell;
Syne the east had a bitter word to say,
    That waukent a watery hell.

He turned her heid intil the north—
    Quo' the nobles, "He s' droon, by the mass!"
Quo' the skipper, "Haud aff yer lady-han's,
    Or ye 'll never see the Bass."

The king creepit doon the cabin-stair
    To drink the gude French wine;

An' up cam' his dochter, the princess fair,
  And luikit ower the brine.

She turned her face to the drivin' snaw,
  To the snaw but and the weet;
It claucht her snood, an' awa like a clud
  Her hair drave oot i' the sleet.

She turned her face to the drivin' win'—
  " Quhat 's that aheid ?" quo' she.
The skipper he threw himsel' frae the win',
  And he drove the helm alee.

" Put to yer han' my lady fair!
  Haud up her heid," quo' he ;
" Gin she dinna face the win' a wee mair
  It 's the waur for you and me."

To the tiller the lady she laid her han',
  And the ship laid her cheek to the blast;
They joukit the berg, but her quarter scraped,
  An' they luikit at ither aghast.

Quo' the skipper, " Ye are a lady fair,
  An' a princess gran' to see;
But war ye a milkmaid, a man wad sail
  To hell i' yer company."

She liftit a pale an' a queenly face:
  Her een flashed, and syne they swam
" And what for no to the lift ?" she says—
  And she turned awa frae him.   .

Bot she took na her han' frae the gude ship's helm
  Till the day began to daw;
And the skipper he spak, but what was said
  It was said atween them twa.

And syne the gude ship she lay to,
 Wi' Scotlan' far un'er the lee;
And the king cam' up the cabin-stair
 Wi' wan face and bluid-shot e'e.

Laigh loutit the skipper upo' the deck;
 "Stan' up, stan' up," quo' the king,
"Ye 're an honest loun—an' ask me a boon
 Quhan ye gi'e me back this ring."

Lowne blew the win', the stars cam' oot,
 The ship turned frae the north;
An' or ever the sun was up' an aboot
 They war intil the firth o' Forth.

Quhan the gude ship hung at the pier-heid,
 And the king stude steady on the lan'—
"Doon wi' ye, skipper—doon !" he said,
 "Hoo daur ye afore me stan'?"

The skipper he louted on his knee,
 The king his blade he drew;
Quo' the king, "Hoo daured ye contre me?—
 I 'm aboord my ain ship noo!

"Gin I hadna been yer verra gude lord,
 I wad ha'e thrawn yer neck!
Bot—ye wha loutit Skipper o' Doon,
 Rise up Yerl o' Waterydeck."

The skipper he raisena,—"Yer grace is great;
 Yer will can heize or ding;
Wi' ae wee word ye ha'e made me a yerl—
 Wi' anither mak' me a king."

"I canna mak' ye a king," quo' he,
 "The Lord alane can do that;
I snowk leise-majesty, my man !
 What the deevil wad ye be at?"

Glowert at the skipper the doutsum king,
   Jalousin' aneth his croon;
Quo' the skipper, "Here is yer grace's ring,
   An' yer dochter is my boon."

The black blood shot intil the king's face—
   He wasna bonny to see;
"The rascal skipper! he lichtlies oor grace!—
   Gar hang him heigh on yon tree."

Up sprang the skipper an' aboord his ship,
   He caught up a bitin' blade;
He hackit at the cable that held her to the pier,
   An' he thocht it ower weel made.

The king he blew hard in a siller whustle;
   An' tramp, tramp, doon the pier
Cam' twenty horsemen on twenty horses,
   Clankin' wi' spur and spear.

At the king's fit fell his dochter fair—
   "His life ye wadna spill!"
"Daur ye to sunder me and my hate?"
   "I daur, wi' a richt gude will!"

"Ye was aye to yer faither a thrawart bairn;
   But, my lady, I am yer king;
An' ye daurna luik me i' the face,
   For a monarch's anither thing."

"I lout to my faither for his grace,
   Low on my bendit knee;
But I stan' and luik the king i' the face,
   For the skipper is king o' me."

She turned; she sprang upo' the deck;
   The cable splashed i' the Forth;
Her wings sae braid the gude ship spread,
   And flew east and syne flew north.

Now was not this a king's dochter—
A lady that feared no skaith—
An' a woman wi' quhilk a man micht sail
Prood intill the port o' Death?
By permission of Messrs. Strahan & Co.

FROM A CHILD'S DIARY.

THE child here is Marjorie Fleming, from the "lang toun," a precocious little angel, who spent seven years and eleven months in this world, and then—

> " She set as sets the morning star, which goes
> Not down behind the darkened west, nor hides
> Obscured among the tempests of the sky,
> But melts away into the light of heaven."

An article, entitled "Marjorie Fleming," appeared in the *North British Review*, some eight or nine years ago, from the charmed pen of Dr. John Brown, in which the short life of the child was graphically sketched. Extracts from a diary kept by her at one time were given; and from these we take the following *morceaux*, with a word or two from Dr. John here and there* :—

" The day of my existence here 'has been delightful and enchanting. On Saturday I expected no less than three well-made Bucks the names of whom is here advertised. Mr. Geo. Crakey (Craigie), and Wm. Keith and Jn. Keith—the first is the funniest of every one of them. Mr. Crakey and walked to Crakyhall (Cragiehall) hand in hand in Innocence and matitation (meditation) sweet thinking on the kind love which flows in our tender hearted mind which is overflowing with majestic pleasure

* Marjorie's words are misspelt and omitted as in the original.

no one was ever so polite to me in the hole state of my existence. Mr. Craky you must know is a great Buck and pretty good-looking.

"I am at Ravelston enjoying nature's fresh air. The birds are singing sweetly—the calf doth frisk and nature shows her glorious face."

Here is a confession:—"I confess I have been very more like a little young divil than a creature for when Isabella went up stairs to teach me religion and my multiplication and to be good and all my other lessons I stamped with my foot and threw my new hat which she had made on the ground and was sulky and was dreadfully passionate, but she never whiped me but said Marjory go into another room and think what a great great crime you are committing letting your temper git the better of you. But I went so sulkily that the Devil got the better of me but she never never whips me so that I think I would be the better of it and the next time that I behave ill I think she should do it for she never does it. . . . Isabella has given me praise for checking my temper for I was sulky even when she was kneeling an hole hour teaching me to write."

Our poor little wifie, *she* has no doubts of the personality of the Devil! "Yesterday I behave extremely ill in God's most holy church for I would never attend myself nor let Isabella attend which was a great crime for she often, often tells me that when to or three are geathered together God is in the midst of them, and it was the very same Divil that tempted Job that tempted me I am sure; but he resisted Satan though he had boils and many many other misfortunes which I have escaped. . . . I am now going to tell you the horible and

wretched plaege (plague) that my multiplication gives me
you can't conceive it the most Devilish thing is 8 times 8
and 7 times 7 it is what nature itself cant endure."

This is delicious; and what harm is there in her
"Devilish?" it is strong language merely; even old
Rowland Hill used to say " he grudged the Devil those
rough and ready words." " I walked to that delightful
place Crakyhall with a delightful young man beloved by
all his friends espacially by me his loveress, but I must
not talk any more about him for Isa said it is not proper
for to speak of gentalmen but I will never forget him!
. . . I am very very glad that satan has not given
me boils and many other misfortunes—In the holy bible
these words are written that the Devil goes like a roaring
lyon in search of his pray but the lord lets us escape
from him but we " (*pauvre petite!*) " do not strive with
this awfull Spirit. . . . To-day I pronunced a word
which should never come out of a lady's lips it was that
I called John a Impudent Bitch. I will tell you what
made me in so bad a humor is I got one or two of that
bad bad sina (senna) tea to-day,"—a better excuse for
bad humour and bad language than most.

She has been reading the Book of Esther: " It was a
dreadful thing that Haman was hanged on the very gallows which he had prepared for Mordeca to hang him
and his ten sons thereon and it was very wrong and
cruel to hang his sons for they did not commit the
crime; *but then Jesus was not then come to teach us to be
merciful.*" This is wise and beautiful—has upon it the
very dew of youth and of holiness. Out of the mouths
of babes and sucklings He perfects His praise.

" This is Saturday and I am very glad of it because I

have play half the Day and I get money too but alas I owe Isabella 4 pence for I am finned 2 pence whenever I bite my nails. Isabella is teaching me to make simme colings nots of interrigations peorids commoes, etc. . . . As this is Sunday I will meditate upon Senciable and Religious subjects. First I should be very thankful I am not a beggar."

This amount of meditation and thankfulness seems to have been all she was able for.

" I am going to-morrow to a delightful place, Braehead by name, belonging to Mrs. Crraford, where there is ducks cocks hens bubblyjocks 2 dogs 2 cats and swine which is delightful. I think it is shocking to think that the dog and cat should bear them " (this is a meditation physiological), " and they are drowned after all. I would rather have a man-dog than a woman-dog, because they do not bear like women-dogs; it is a hard case—it is shocking. I cam here to enjoy natures delightful breath it is sweeter than a fial (phial) of rose oil."

This is beautiful :—" I am very sorry to say that I forgot God—that is to say I forgot to pray to-day and Isabella told me that I should be thankful that God did not forget me—if he did, O what become of me if I was in danger and God not friends with me—I must go to unquench-able fire and if I was tempted to sin—how could I resist it O no I will never do it again—no no—if I can help it." (Canny wee wifie!) " My religion is greatly falling off because I dont pray with so much attention when I am saying my prayers, and my charecter is lost among the Braehead people. I hope I will be religious again— but as for regaining my charecter I despair for it." (Poor little " habit and repute !")

K

Her temper, her passion, and her "badness" are almost daily confessed and deplored:—"I will never again trust to my own power, for I see that I cannot be good without God's assistance—I will not trust in my own selfe, and Isa's health will be quite ruined by me— it will indeed." "Isa has giving me advice, which is, that when I feal Satan beginning to tempt me, that I flea him and he would flea me." "Remorse is the worst thing to bear, and I am afraid that I will fall a marter to it."

Poor dear little sinner!—here comes the world again: "In my travels I met with a handsome lad named Charles Balfour Esq., and from him I got offers of marage —offers of marage, did I say? Nay plenty heard me." A fine scent for "breach of promise!"

This is abrupt and strong:—"The Divil is curced and all works. 'Tis a fine work *Newton on the profecies*. I wonder if there is another book of poems comes near the Bible. The Divil always girns at the sight of the Bible." "Miss Potune" (her "simpliton" friend) "is very fat; she pretends to be very learned. She says she saw a stone that dropt from the skies; but she is a good Christian." Here come her views on church government:— "An Annibabtist is a thing I am not a member of—I am a Pisplekan (Episcopalian) just now, and" (Oh you little Laodicean and Latitudinarian!) "a Prisbetcran at Kirkcaldy!"—(*Blandula! Vagula! cœlum et animum mutas quæ trans mare* (i.e., *trans Bodotriam*)-*curris!*)—"my native town." "Sentiment is not what I am acquainted with as yet, though I wish it, and should like to practise it" (!) "I wish I had a great, great deal of gratitude in my heart, in all my body." "There is a new novel published, named *Self-Control*" (Mrs. Brunton's)—"a very good maxim forsooth!" This is shocking: "Yesterday a marrade man, named Mr. John Balfour, Esq., offered to kiss me, and offered to marry me, though the man" (a fine directness this!) "was espused, and his wife was present and said he must ask her permission; but he did not. I think he was ashamed and confounded before 3 gentelman—Mr. Jobson and 2 Mr. Kings." "Mr. Ban-ester's" (Bannister's) "Budjet is to-night; I hope it will be a good one. A great many authors have expressed themselves too sentimentally." You are right, Marjorie. "A Mr. Burns writes a beautiful song on Mr. Cunhaming, whose wife desarted him—truly it is a most beautiful one." "I like to read the Fabulous historys, about the histerys of Robin, Dickey, flapsay, and Peccay, and it is very amusing, for some were good birds and others bad, but Peccay was the most dutiful and obedient to her parients." "Thomson is a beautiful author, and Pope, but nothing to Shakespear, of which I have a little knolege. *Macbeth* is a pretty composition, but awful one." "The *Newgate Calender* is very instructive" (!) "A sailor called here to say farewell; it must be dreadful to leave his native country when he might get a wife; or perhaps me, for I love him very much. But O I forgot, Isabella forbid me to speak about love." This antiphlogistic regimen and lesson is ill to learn by our Maidie, for here she sins again:—"Love is a very papithatick thing" (it is almost a pity to correct this into pathetic), "as well as troublesome and tiresome—but O Isabella forbid me to speak of it." Here are her reflections on a pine-apple:— "I think the price of a pine-apple is very dear: it is a whole bright goulden guinea, that might have sustained

a poor family." Here is a new vernal simile:—"The
hedges are sprouting like chicks from the eggs when they
are newly hatched or, as the vulgar say, *clacked.*" " Doctor Swift's works are very funny; I got some of them by
heart." " Moreheads sermons are I hear much praised,
but I never read sermons of any kind; but I read
novelettes and my Bible, and I never forget it, or my
prayers." Bravo Marjorie!

By permission of Dr. Brown.

WEE JOUKYDAIDLES.*

BY JAMES SMITH.

WEE Joukydaidles,
   Toddlin' oot an' in:
Oh, but she's a cutty,
   Makin' sic a din!
Aye sae fou' o' mischief,
   And minds na what I say:
My very heart gangs loup, loup,
   Fifty times a day!

Wee Joukydaidles—
   Where's the stumpie noo?
She's tumblin' i' the cruivie,
   An' lauchin' to the soo!
Noo she sees my angry ee,
   An' aff she's like a hare!
Lassie, when I get ye,
   I'll scud ye till I'm sair!

* From *Poems, Songs, and Ballads;* third edition. Blackwood & Sons,
Edinburgh and London.

Wee Joukydaidles—
  Noo she's breakin' dishes—
Noo she's soakit i' the burn,
  Catchin' little fishes;
Noo she's i' the barn-yard,
  Playin' wi' the fouls—
Feeding them wi' butter-cakes,
  Snaps, an' sugar-bools.

Wee Joukydaidles—
  Oh, my heart its broke!
She's torn my braw new wincey,
  To mak' a dolly's frock.
There's the goblet ower the fire!
  The jaud! she weel may rin!
No a tattie ready yet,
  An' faither comin' in!

Wee Joukydaidles—
  Wha's sae tired as me!
See! the kettle's doun at last!
  Waes me for my tea!
Oh, it's angersome, atweel,
  An' sune 'll mak' me gray:
My very heart gangs loup, loup,
  Fifty times a day! ·

Wee Joukydaidles—
  Where's the smoukie noo?
She's hidin' i' the coal-hole,
  Cryin' "Keekybo!"
Noo she's at the fireside,
  Pu'in' pussy's tail—
Noo she's at the broun bowl,
  Suppin' a' the kail!

Wee Joukydaidles—
  Paidlin' i' the shower—

There she's at the wundy,
    Haud her, or she's ower!
Noo she's slippit frae my sicht:
    Where's the wean at last?
In the byre amang the kye,
    Sleepin' soun' an' fast!

Wee Joukydaidles—
    For a' ye gi'e me pain,
Ye're aye my darlin' tottie yet—
    My ain wee wean!
An' gin I'm spared to ither days—
    Oh, may they come to pass—
I'll see my bonnie bairnie
    A braw, braw lass!

OLD AGE.

By Mrs. Elizabeth Hamilton.

Is that Old Age that's tirling at the pin?
I trow it is—then haste to let him in.
Ye're kindly welcome, friend; na, dinna fear
To show yoursel', ye'll cause nae trouble here.
I ken there are wha tremble at your name,
As though ye brought wi' ye reproach or shame;.
And wha "o' thousand lies would bear the sin,"
Rather than own ye for their kith or kin?
But far frae shirking ye as a disgrace,
Thankfu' I am to have lived to see yer face;
Nor sall I e'er disown ye, nor tak' pride
To think how long I might yer visit bide;
Doing my best to mak' ye weel respected,
I'll no for your sake, fear to be neglected;
But now ye're come, and through a' kind o' weather

We 're doomed, frae this time forth, to jog together,
I'd fain mak' compact wi' ye, firm and strang,
On terms of fair giff-gaff to haud out lang·
Gin thou 'lt be civil, I sall liberal be—
Witness the lang, lang list of what I 'll gi'e.

First, then, I here mak' ower, for gude and aye,
A' youthfu' fancies, whether bright or gay;
Beauties and graces, too, I wad resign 'em,
But sair, I fear, 'twad cost ye fash to find 'em:
For, 'gainst your daddy, Time, they couldna stand,
Nor bear the grip o' his unsonsy hand.
But there 's my skin, whilk ye may further crunkle,
And write yer name at length in ilka wrunkle;
On my brown locks ye 've leave to lay yer paw,
And bleach them to yer fancy, white as snaw.
But luk' na', Age, sae wistfu' at my mouth,
As gin ye longed to pu' out ilka tooth.
Let them, I do beseech, still keep their places,
Though, gin ye wish, ye 're free to paint their faces.
My limbs I yield ye; and if ye see meet
To clasp yer icy shackles on my feet,
I 'll no refuse; but if ye drive out gout,
Will bless ye for 't, and offer thanks devout.
Sae muckle wad I gi'e wi' right gude will;
But, oh! I fear that mair ye look for still.
I ken by that fell glower and meaning shrug,
Ye'd clap yer skinny fingers on each lug,
And unco fain ye are, I trow, and keen
To cast yer misty pooders in my een.
But, oh! in mercy spare my poor wee twinkers,
An' I for aye sall wear your crystal blinkers;
Then, 'bout my lugs, I 'd fain a bargain mak',
And gi'e my han' that I shall ne'er draw back.
Well, then, wad ye consent their use to share?
'Twad serve us baith, and be a bargain rare.
Thus I wad hae 't—when babbling fools intrude,
Gabbling their noisy nonsense, lang and loud;

Or when ill-nature, weel brushed up by wit,
Wi' sneer sarcastic takes its aim to hit;
Or when detraction—meanest slave o' pride—
Spies out wee fau'ts, and seeks great worth to hide;
Then mak' me deaf, as deaf as deaf can be:
At a' sic times my lugs I'll lend to thee.
But when in social hour ye see combined
Genius and wisdom, fruits o' heart and mind,
Good sense, good humor, wit in playfu' mood,
And candour e'en frae ill extracting good;
Oh, then, auld friend, I maun ha'e back my hearin',
To want it then wad be an ill past bearin';
Better to lonely sit i' the doaf spence,
Than catch the sough of words without the sense.
Ye winna promise? Oh, ye're unco dour,
Sae ill to manage, and sae cauld and sour.
Nae matter; hale and sound I'll keep my heart,
Nor frae a crumb o't sall I ever part;
Its kindly warmth will ne'er be chill'd by a'
The cauldest breath your frozen lips can blaw.
Ye need na' fash yer thum', auld carl, nor fret,
For there affection shall preserve its seat;
And though to tak' my hearin' ye rejoice,
Yet spite o' you I'll still hear friendship's voice:
Thus, though ye tak' the rest, it sha' na' grieve me,
For ae blithe spunk o' spirits ye maun leave me.
And let me tell ye in yer lug, Auld Age,
I'm bound to travel wi' ye but ane stage;
Be't long or short, ye canna keep me back,
And when we reach the end o't, ye maun pack;
For there we part for ever; late or air,
Another guess companion meets me there,
To whom ye, will ye, nill ye, maun me bring,
Nor think that I'll be wae, or loth to spring
Frae your poor doomed side, ye carl uncouth,
To the blest arms of everlasting youth;
By him, whate'er ye've rifled, stolen, or ta'en,
Will a' be given wi' interest back again.

Ye need na' wonder, then, nor swell with pride,
Because I kindly welcome you as guide
To ane sae far your better.   Now a 's tauld,
Let us set out upon our journey cauld,
Wi' nae vain boasts nor vain regrets tormented,
We 'll e'en jog on the gate, pleased and contented.

DONALD MACLEOD.

DONALD MACLEOD!   Would'st hear his story told?
No stormy legend of the days of old,
Of war, and tournament, and high emprize,
Or knightly feuds beneath fair ladies' eyes;
But a true story of our modern time,
Such as befel, in cold Canadian clime
A dozen winters past.   Donald MacLeod,
A poor man—one of millions—in the crowd.

A stalwart wight he was, whom but to see
Were to wish friend rather than enemy;
A smith by trade, a bluff, hard-working man,
Proud of his sires, his race, his name, his clan.'
His strong right arm could hurl a foeman down
Like ball a skittle; his broad brow was brown
With honest toil, and in his clear blue eye
Lurked strength to conquer fortune or defy.
Few were his words, and those but rough at best,
But truthful ever as his own true breast;
Of homely nature, not of winning ways,
Or given to tears, or overmuch of praise;
But with a heart as guileless as a child's
Of seven years old, that frolics in the wilds.

Ere Donald left his shieling in the glen,
By the burn-side that tumbles down the Ben

On gray Lochaber's melancholy shore,
And sighed, like others, " I return no more,"
To try his fortune in the fight of life
In a new world, with fairer field for strife
Than Scotland offers, overfilled with brains,
Yet scant of acres to reward their pains,
He woo'd with simple speech a Highland maid,
Sweet as the opening flow'ret in the shade,
And asked her, " Would she quit her native land,
Her mother's love, her father's guiding.hand,
And make another sunshine far away,
For him alone?" She blessed the happy day
That a good man, so honest and so brave,
Had sought the heart and hand she freely gave.
To see the pair, the man so massive strong,
The maid so frail, yet winsome as a song,
You might have thought the oak had chosen for bride
The gowan, glinting on the green hill-side.

And Jeannie Cameron! happy wife was she,
Sailing with Donald o'er the summer sea,
And dreaming, as the good ship cleft the foam,
Of independence and a happy home,
On that abundant and rejoicing soil
That asks but hands to recompense their toil.
And Fortune favoured them, as Fortune will
All who add strength and virtue to good-will.
And Donald's hands found always work to do,
Work well repaid, which, growing, ever grew;
Work and its fair reward but seldom known
In the old land, whence hopeful he had flown;
Work all sufficient for the passing day,
With something left to hoard and put away.
Content and Donald never dwelt apart,
And love and Jeannie nestled at his heart.

In summer eves, his face towards the sun,
He loved to sit, his long day's labour done,

And smoke his pipe beneath the sycamore,
That cast cool shadow at his cottage door,
And hear his bonny Jean, like morning lark
Or nightingale preluding to the dark,
Sing the old Gaelic melancholy songs
Of Scotland's glory, Scotland's rights and wrongs,
Of true-love ditties of the olden time,
Breathing of Highland glens and moorland thyme.

Thus years wore on.   Their sky seemed sunny blue,
Without a cloud to shade the distant view
Of happiness to come.   A child was born,
Fresh to the father's heart as light of morn,
Sweet to the mother's as a dream of heaven,
A blessing asked, but scarcely hoped when given.
Most dearly prized!   Alas! for human joy,
That Fortune never builds but to destroy!
The child was purchased by the mother's health!
And Donald's heart grew heavy, as by stealth
He gazed and saw the sadness in her smile
That lit, yet half extinguished it the while;
For, ah! poor Jeannie was too fair and frail
To bear unscathed Canadia's wintry gale;
And hectic roses flourished on her cheek,
Filling his heart with grief, too great to speak.
Long, long, he watched her, and essayed to find
Comfort and hope.   At last upon his mind
Burst suddenly the thought that he 'd forego
All he had earned in that New World of woe,
And bear her back, ere utterly forlorn,
To the moist mountain clime where she was born,—
To dear Lochaber and the Highland hills,
And wave-invaded glens and wimpling rills,
Where first he found her.   Late, alas! too late!

"Donald," she said, "I feel approaching fate,
And may not travel o'er the stormy sea,
To die on shipboard and be torn from thee;

Here let me linger till I go to rest!
Time may be short or long, God knoweth best.
But as the tree that's planted in the ground,
And sheds its blossoms and its leaves around,
Dies where it lives, so let me live and die
Where thou hast brought me, 'twixt the earth and sky.
I'd not be buried in the Atlantic wave,
But in brown earth, with daisies on my grave;
Fresh blooming gowans from Lochaber's braes,
With Scottish earth enough, the mound to raise
Above my head.　Donald! let this be done
When your poor Jeannie's mortal race is run!"

'The strong man wept,　"Jeannie!" was all he said.
"O Jeannie! Jeannie!" and he bowed his head,
And hid his face behind his honest hands,
The saddest man in all those happy lands.
"Jeannie!" he said, "ye maunna, maunna dee,
And leave the world to misery and me!"

"Donald!" she answered, "woeful is the strife,
That my warm heart is fighting for its life;
And much as I desire for thy dear sake,
And the wee bairn's, to live till age o'er-take,
I feel it cannot be.　God's will is all,—
Let us accept it, whatsoe'er befall!"

And Jeannie died.　She had not lain i' the mools
Three days ere Donald laid aside his tools,
And closed his forge, and took his passage home
To Glasgow, for Lochaber o'er the foam.
Alone with sorrow and alone with love,
The two but one to lead his heart above;
And long ere forty days had ran their round,
Donald was back upon Canadian ground—
Donald, the tender heart, the rough, the brave—
With earth and gowans for his true love's grave.

From " All the Year Round," by permission of Charles Dickens, Esq.

THE WEE WIFUKIE.

BY THE REV. ALEXANDER GEDDES, ROMAN CATHOLIC
CLERGYMAN, BANFF, BORN 1737, DIED 1802.

THERE was a wee bit wifukie was comin' frae the fair,
Had got a wee bit drappukie that bred her meikle care:
It gaed about the wifie's heart, and she began to spew,—
"Oh!" quo' the wee wifukie, "I wish I binna fou.

"If Johnnie find me barley-sick, I'm sure he'll claw my skin;
But I'll lay down and tak' a nap before that I gae in."
Sitting at the dyke-side, and taking o' her nap,
By cam' a packman laddie wi' a little pack.

He's clippit a' her gowden locks, sae bonny and sae lang;
He's ta'en her purse and a' her placks, and fast awa he ran;
And when the wifie waken'd, her head was like a bee,—
"Oh!" quo' the wee wifukie, "this is nae me.

"I met with kindly company, and birl'd my bawbee;
And still, if this be Bessukie, three placks remain wi' me;
But I will look the pursie nooks, see gin the cunyie be,—
There's neither purse nor plack about me! this is nae me.

"I ha'e a little housikie, but an' a kindly man;
A dog, they ca' him Doussikie—if this be me, he'll fawn;
And Johnnie, he'll come to the door, and kindly welcome me,
And a' the bairns on the floorhead will dance, if this be me."

The night was late, and dang out weel, and oh! but it was dark—
The doggie heard a body's foot, and he began to bark.
Oh! when she heard the doggie bark, and kennin' it was she,
"Oh! weel ken ye, Doussikie," quo' she, "this is nae me."

When Johnnie heard his Bessie's word, fast to the door he ran,—
"Is that you Bessukie?" "How na, man.

Be kind to the bairns a', and weel mat ye be;
And farewell, Johnnie," quo' she, "this is nae me."

John ran to the minister—his hair stood a' on end,—
"I 've gotten sic a fright, sir, I fear I 'll never mend:
My wife 's come home without a head, crying out most piteously,
'Oh, farewell, Johnnie,' quo' she, 'this is nae me.'"

"The tale you tell," the parson said, "is wonderful to me,
How that a wife without a head could speak, or hear, or see!
But things that happen hereabout, so strangely alter'd be,
That I could maist wi' Bessie say, 'tis neither you nor she."

Now Johnnie, he cam' hame again, and oh! but he was fain
To see his little Bessukie come to hersel' again.
He got her sitting on a stool, wi' Tibbuck on her knee.
"Oh! come awa, Johnnie," quo' she, "come awa to me,
For I 've got a nap wi' Tibbuckie, and this is now me."

ROBERT FALCONER'S PLAN OF SALVATION.

By George MacDonald, M.A., LL.D.

Robert began to take fits of soul-saving, a most
rational exercise, worldly wise and prudent—right too
on the principles he had received, but not in the least
Christian in its nature, or even God-fearing. His
imagination began to busy itself in representing the dire
consequences of not entering into the one refuge of faith.
He made many frantic efforts to believe that he believed;
took to keeping the Sabbath very carefully—that is, by
going to church three times, and to Sunday-school, as
well; by never walking a step save to or from church;
by never saying a word upon any subject unconnected
with religion, chiefly theoretical; by never reading any

but religious books; by never whistling; by never thinking of his lost fiddle, and so on—all the time feeling
that God was ready to pounce upon him if he failed
once; till again and again the intensity of his efforts
utterly defeated their object by destroying for the time
the desire to prosecute them with the power to will
them. But througn the horrible vapours of these vain
endeavours, which denied God altogether as the maker
of the world, and the former of his soul and heart and
brain, and sought to worship Him as a capricious demon,
there broke a little light, a little soothing, soft twilight,
from the dim windows of such literature as came in his
way. Besides *The Pilgrim's Progress*, there were several
books which shone moon-like on his darkness, and lifted
something of the weight of that Egyptian gloom off his
spirit. One of these, strange to say, was Defoe's
Religious Courtship, and one, Young's *Night Thoughts*.
But there was another which deserves particular notice,
inasmuch as it did far more than merely interest or amuse
him, raising a deep question in his mind, and one worthy
to be asked. This book was the translation of Klop-
stock's *Messiah*, to which I have already referred. It
was not one of his grandmother's books, but had probably belonged to his father: he had found it in his
little garret room. But as often as she saw him reading it,
she seemed rather pleased, he thought. As to the book
itself, its florid expatiation could neither offend nor
injure a boy like Robert, while its representation of our
Lord was to him a wonderful relief from that given in
the pulpit, and in all the religious books he knew. But
the point for the sake of which I refer to it in particular
is this: amongst the rebel angels who are of the actors

in the story, one of the principal is a cherub who repents of making his choice with Satan, mourns over his apostasy, haunts unseen the steps of our Saviour, wheels lamenting about the cross, and would gladly return to his lost duties in heaven, if only he might—a doubt which I ˙ believe is left unsolved in the volume, and naturally enough remained unsolved in Robert's mind:— Would poor Abbadon be forgiven and taken home again? For although naturally—that is, to judge by his own instincts—there could be no question of his forgiveness, according to what he had been taught, there could be no question of his perdition. Having no one to talk to, he divided himself and went to buffets on the subject, siding, of course, with the better half of himself which supported the merciful view of the matter; for all his efforts at keeping the Sabbath had, in his own honest judgment, failed so entirely that he had no ground for believing himself one of the elect. Had he succeeded in persuading himself that he was, there is no saying to what lengths of indifference about others the chosen prig might have advanced by this time.

He made one attempt to open the subject with Shargar.

" Shargar, what think ye?" he said suddenly, one day. " Gin a de'il war to repent, wad God forgie him?"

" There's no sayin' what fowk wad du till ance they're tried," returned Shagar, cautiously.

Robert did not care to resume the question with one who so circumspectly refused to take a metaphysical or *a priori* view of the matter.

He made an attempt with his grandmother.

One Sunday, his thoughts, after trying for a time to

revolve in due orbit around the mind of the Rev. Hugh MacCleary, as projected in a sermon which he had botched up out of a commentary, failed at last, and flew off into what the said gentleman would have pronounced "very dangerous speculation, seeing no man is to go beyond what is written in the Bible, which contains not only the truth, but the whole truth, and nothing but the truth, for this time and for all future time—both here and in the world to come." Some such sentence, at least, was in his sermon that day; and the preacher no doubt supposed St. Matthew, not Matthew Henry, accountable for its origination. In the Limbo into which Robert's then spirit flew, it had been sorely exercised about the substitution of the sufferings of Christ for those which humanity must else have endured while ages rolled on— mere ripples on the ocean of eternity.

"Noo, be douce," said Mrs. Falconer, solemnly, as Robert, a trifle lighter at heart from the result of his cogitations than usual, sat down to dinner: he had happened to smile across the table to Shargar. And he was douce, and smiled no more.

They ate their broth, or, more properly, *supped* it, with horn spoons, in absolute silence; after which Mrs. Falconer put a large piece of meat on the plate of each, with the same formula:

"Hae. Ye's get nae mair."

The allowance was ample in the extreme, bearing a relation to her words similar to that which her practice bore to her theology. A piece of cheese, because it was the Sabbath, followed, and dinner was over.

When the table had been cleared by Betty, they drew their chairs to the fire, and Robert had to read to his

I!

grandmother, while Shargar sat listening. He had not read long, however, before he looked up from his Bible and began the following conversation:—

" Wasna it an ill trick o' Joseph, gran'mither, to put that cup, an' a siller ane tu, into the mou' o' Benjamin's seck?"

" What for that, laddie? He wanted to gar them come back again, ye ken."

" But he needna ha'e gane aboot in sic a playactor-like gait. He needna ha'e latten them awa ohn telt (*without telling*) them that he was their brither."

" They had behaved verra ill till him."

" He used to clype (*tell tales*) upo' them, though."

" Laddie, tak' ye care what ye say aboot Joseph, for he was a teep o' Christ."

" Hoo was that, gran'mither?"

" They sellt him to the Ishmelects for siller, as Judas did Him."

" Did he beir the sins o' them 'at sellt him?"

" Ye may say, in a mainner, 'at he did; for he was sair afflickit afore he wan up to be the King's richt han'; an' syne he keepit a hantle o' ill aff o' 's brithren."

" Sae, gran'mither, ither fowk nor Christ micht suffer for the sins o' their neebors?"

" Ay, laddie, mony a ane has to do that. But no to mak' atonement, ye ken. Naething but the sufferin' o' the spotless cud du that. The Lord wadna be saitisfeet wi' less nor that. It maun be the innocent to suffer for the guilty."

" I unnerstan' that," said Robert, who had heard it so often that he had not yet thought of trying to understand it. " But gin we gang to the gude place, we'll be a' innocent, willna we, grannie?"

"Ay, that we will—washed spotless and pure, and clean, and dressed i' the weddin' garment, and set doon at the table wi' Him and wi' His Father. That's them 'at believes in Him, ye ken."

"Of coorse, grannie. Weel, ye see, I ha'e been thinkin' o' a plan for maist han' toomin' (*almost emptying*) hell."

"What's i' the bairn's heid noo? Troth, ye're no blate, meddlin' wi' sic subjecks, laddie!"

"I didna want to say onything to vex ye, grannie. I s' gang on wi' the chapter."

"Ow, say awa. Ye sanna say muckle 'at's wrang afore I cry *haud*," said Mrs. Falconer, curious to know what had been moving in the boy's mind, but watching him like a cat, ready to spring upon the first visible hair of the old Adam.

And Robert, recalling the outbreak of terrible grief which he had heard on that memorable night, really thought that his project would bring comfort to a mind burdened with such care, and went on with the exposition of his plan.

"A' them 'at sits doon to the supper o' the Lamb 'll sit there because Christ suffert the punishment due to their sins—winna they, grannie?"

"Doobtless, laddie."

"But it'll be some sair upo' them to sit there aitin' an' drinkin' an' talkin' awa, an' enjoyin' themsel's, whan ilka noo an' than there'll come a sough o' wailin' up frae the ill place, an' a smell o' burnin' ill to bide."

"What put that i' yer heid, laddie? There's no rizzon to think 'at hell's sae near haven as a' that. The Lord forbid it!"

"Weel, but, grannie, they'll ken't a' the same, whether

they smell't or no. An' I canna help thinkin' that the
farrer awa I thoucht they war, the waur I wad like to
think upo' them. 'Deed it wad be waur."

"What are ye drivin' at, laddie? I canna unnerstan
ye," said Mrs. Falconer, feeling very uncomfortable, and
yet curious, almost anxious, to hear what would come
next. "I trust we winna ha'e to think muckle——"

But here, I presume, the thought of the added desola-
tion of her Andrew, if she, too, were to forget him, as
well as his Father in heaven, checked the flow of her
words. She paused, and Robert took up his parable and
went on, first with yet another question.

"Duv ye think, grannie, that a body wad be allooed
to speik a word i' public, like, there—at the lang table,
like, I mean?"

"What for no, gin it was dune wi' moedesty, and for
a gude rizzon? But railly, laddie, I doobt ye're haverin'
a'thegither. Ye heard naething like that, I'm sure, the
day, frae Mr. MacCleary."

"Na, na; he said naething aboot it. But maybe I'll
gang and speir at him, though."

"What aboot?"

"What I'm gaein' to tell ye, grannie."

"Weel, tell awa, and ha'e dune wi''t. I'm growin'
tired o''t."

It was something else than tired she was growing.

"Weel, I'm gaein' to try a' that I can to win in
there."

"I houp ye will. Strive and pray. Resist the deevil.
Walk i' the licht. Lippen not to yersel', but trust in
Christ and His salvation."

"Ay, ay, grannie. Weel——"

"Are ye no dune yet?"

"Na.   I'm but jist beginnin'."

"Beginnin' are ye?   Humph!"

"Weel, gin I win in there, the verra first nicht I sit down wi' the lave o' them, I'm gaein' to rise up an' say —that is, gin the Maister at the heid o' the table disna bid me sit doon—an' say: 'Brithers an' sisters, the haill o' ye, hearken to me for ae minute; an', O Lord! gin I say wrang, jist tak' the speech frae me, an' I'll sit doon dumb an' rebukit.   We're a' here by grace and no by merit, save His, as ye a' ken better nor I can tell ye, for ye ha'e been langer here nor me.   But it's jist ruggin' an rivin' at my hert to think o' them 'at's doon there. Maybe ye can hear them.   I canna.   Noo, we ha'e nae merit, an' they ha'e nae merit, an' what for are we here and them there?   But we're washed clean and innocent noo; and noo, whan there's no wyte lying upo' oursel's, it seems to me that we micht beir some o' the sins o' them 'at ha'e ower mony.   I call upo' ilk' ane o' ye 'at has a frien' or a neebor down yonner, to rise up an' taste nor bite nor sup mair till we gang up a' thegither to the fut o' the throne, and pray the Lord to lat's gang and du as the Maister did afore's, and bier their griefs, and carry their sorrows doon in hell there; gin it maybe that they may repent and get remission o' their sins, an' come up here wi' us at the lang last, and sit doon wi''s at this table, a' throuw the merits o' oor Saviour Jesus Christ, at the heid o' the table there.   Amen.'"

Half ashamed of his long speech, half overcome by the feelings fighting within him, and altogether bewildered, Robert burst out crying like a baby, and ran out of the room—up to his own place of meditation, where he threw

himself upon the floor. Shargar, who had made neither
head nor tail of it all, as he said afterwards, sat staring
at Mrs. Falconer. She rose, and going into Robert's
little bedroom, closed the door, and what she did there
is not far to seek.

When she came out, she rang the bell for tea, and
sent Shargar to look for Robert. When he appeared,
she was so gentle to him that it woke quite a new sensation
in him. But after tea was over, she said,—

"Noo, Robert, let's ha'e nae mair o' this. Ye ken as
weel 's I du that them 'at gangs *there* their doom is fixed,
and noething *can* alter 't. An' we 're not to alloo oor ain
fancies to cairry 's ayont Scripter. We ha'e oor ain
salvation to work oot wi' fear an' trimlin'. We ha'e
naething to do wi' what 's hidden. Luik ye till 't 'at ye
win in yersel'. That 's eneuch for you to min'. Shargar,
ye can gang to the kirk. Robert 's to bide wi' me the
nicht."

Mrs. Falconer very rarely went to church; for she
could not hear a word, and found it irksome.

When Robert and she were alone together,—

"Laddie," she said, "be ye waure o' judgin' the Al-
michty. What luiks to you a' wrang may be a' richt.
But it 's true eneuch 'at we dinna ken a' thing; an' he 's
no deid yet—I dinna believe 'at he is—and he 'll maybe
win in yet."

Here her voice failed her. And Robert had nothing
to say now. He had said all his say before.

"Pray, Robert, pray for yer father, laddie," she
resumed; "for we ha'e muckle rizzon to be anxious
aboot 'im. Pray while there 's life an' houp. Gie the
Lord no rist. Pray till 'im day an' nicht, as I du, that

He wad lead 'im to see the error o' his ways, an' turn to the Lord, wha's ready to pardon. Gin yer mother had lived, I wad ha'e had mair houp, I confess; for she was a braw leddy, an' a bonny, and *that* sweet-tongued! She cud ha'e wiled a maukin frae its lair wi' her bonny Hielan' speech. I never likit to hear nane o' them speyk the Erse (*Irish*, that is *Gaelic*), it was aye sae gloggie and baneless; and I▪cudna unnerstan' ae word o' 't. Nae mair cud yer father—hoot! yer gran'father, I mean—though his father cud speyk it weel. But to hear yer mother—mamma, as ye used to ca' her aye, efter the new fashion—to hear her speyk English, that was sweet to the ear; for the braid Scotch she kent as little o' as I do o' the Erse. It was hert's care aboot him that shortent her days. And a' that'll be laid upo' him. He'll ha'e't a' to beir an accoont for. Och hone! och hone! Eh, Robert, my man, be a gude lad, an' serve the Lord wi' a' yer hert, an' sowl, an' strength, an' min'! for gin ye gang wrang, yer ain father'll ha'e to beir naebody kens hoo muckle o' the wyte o' 't; for he's dune naething to bring ye up i' the way ye suld gang, an' haud ye oot o' the ill gait. For the sake o' yer puir father, haud ye to the richt road. It may spare him a pang or twa i' the ill place. Eh, gin the Lord wad only tak' me, and lat him gang!"

Involuntarily and unconsciously the mother's love was adopting the hope which she had denounced in her grandson. And Robert saw it; but he was never the man, when I knew him, to push a victory. He said nothing. Only a tear or two at the memory of the wayworn man, his recollection of whose visit I have already recorded, rolled down his cheeks. He was at such a distance from him!—such an impassable gulf yawned between them! that was the grief! Not the gulf of death, nor the gulf that divides hell from heaven, but the gulf of abjuration by the good because of his evil ways. His grandmother, herself weeping fast and silently, with scarce altered countenance, took her neatly-folded handkerchief from her pocket, and wiped her grandson's fresh cheeks, then wiped her own withered face; and from that moment Robert knew that he loved her.

Then followed the Sabbath-evening prayer that she always offered with the boy, whichever he was, who kept her company. They knelt down together, side by side, in a certain corner of the room, the same, I doubt not, in which she knelt at her private devotions, before going to bed. There she uttered a long extempore prayer, rapid in speech, full of divinity and Scripture-phrases, but not the less earnest and simple, for it flowed from a heart of faith. Then Robert had to pray after her, loud in her ear, that she might hear him thoroughly, so that he often felt as if he were praying to her, and not to God at all.

She had began to teach him to pray so early that the custom reached beyond the confines of his memory. At first he had had to repeat the words after her; but soon she made him construct his own utterances, now and then giving him a suggestion in the form of a petition, when he seemed likely to break down, or putting a phrase into what she considered more suitable language. But all such assistance she had given up long ago.

On the present occasion, after she had ended her petitions with those for Jews and Pagans, and especially for the " Pop' o' Rom'," in whom, with a rare liberality, she took the kindest interest, she turned to Robert with the usual "Noo, Robert;" and Robert began. But after he had gone on for some time with the ordinary phrases, he turned all at once into a new track, and instead of praying in general terms for "those that would not walk in the right way," said,—

"O Lord! save my father," and there paused.

"If it be Thy will," suggested his grandmother.

But Robert continued silent. His grandmother repeated the subjunctive clause.

"I'm tryin', grandmother," said Robert, "but I canna say't. I daurna say an *if* aboot it. It wad be like giein' in till's damnation. We *maun ha'e* him saved, grannie!"

"Laddie! laddie! haud yer tongue!" said Mrs. Falconer, in a tone of distressed awe. "O Lord, forgie 'im. He's young and disna ken better yet. He canna unnerstan' Thy ways, nor, for that maitter, can I preten' to unnerstan' them mysel'. But Thoo art a' licht, and in Thee is no darkness at all. And Thy licht comes into oor blin' een, and mak's them blinner yet. But, O Lord, gin it wad please Thee to hear oor prayer . . . eh! hoo we wad praise Thee! And my Andrew wad praise Thee mair nor ninety and nine o' them 'at need nae repentance."

A long pause followed. And then the only words that would come were: "For Christ's sake. Amen."

When she said that God was light, instead of concluding therefrom that He could not do the deeds of darkness, she was driven, from a faith in the teaching of Jonathan Edwards as implicit as that of "any lay papist of Loretto," to doubt whether the deeds of darkness were not after all deeds of light, or at least to conclude that their character depended not on their own nature, but on who did them.

They rose from their knees, and Mrs. Falconer sat down by her fire, with her feet on her little wooden stool, and began, as was her wont in that household twilight, ere the lamp was lighted, to review her past life, and follow her lost son through all conditions and circumstances to her imaginable. And when the world to come arose before her, clad in all the glories which her fancy, chilled by education and years, could supply, it was but to vanish in the gloom of the remembrance of him with whom she dared not hope to share its blessedness.

From " Robert Falconer," by permission of Messrs. Hurst and Blackett.

THE COTTAR'S SATURDAY NIGHT.

By Robert Burns.

[Inscribed to R. Aiken, Esq.]

" Let not ambition mock their useful toil,
 Their homely joys, and destiny obscure;
 Nor grandeur hear, with a disdainful smile,
 The short but simple annals of the poor."—GRAY.

My lov'd, my honour'd, much respected friend!
No mercenary bard his homage pays;
With honest pride I scorn each selfish end:
My dearest meed, a friend's esteem and praise.
To you I sing, in simple Scottish lays,
The lowly train in life's sequester'd scene ;

The native feelings strong, the guileless ways;
What Aiken in a cottage would have been;
Ah! though his worth unknown, far happier there, I ween.

November chill blaws loud wi' angry sugh;
The shortening winter day is near a close;
The miry beasts retreating frae the pleugh,
The blackening trains o' craws to their repose:
The toil-worn Cottar frae his labour goes,
This night his weekly moil is at an end,
Collects his spades, his mattocks, and his hoes,
Hoping the morn in ease and rest to spend,
And weary, o'er the moor, his course does hameward bend.

At length his lonely cot appears in view,
Beneath the shelter of an aged tree;
The expectant wee-things, toddlin', stacher through
To meet their dad, wi' flichterin' noise an' glee.
His wee bit ingle, blinking bonnily,
His clean hearthstane, his thriftie wifie's smile,
The lisping infant prattling on his knee,
Does a' his weary carking cares beguile,
An' makes him quite forget his labour an' his toil.

Belyve, the elder bairns come drapping in,
At service out, amang the farmers roun':
Some ca' the pleugh, some herd, some tentie rin
A cannie errand to a neebor town:
Their eldest hope, their Jenny, woman grown,
In youthfu' bloom, love sparkling in her e'e,
Comes hame, perhaps, to show a braw new gown,
Or deposite her sair-won penny-fee,
To help her parents dear, if they in hardship be.

Wi' joy unfeign'd brothers and sisters meet,
An' each for other's welfare kindly speirs:
The social hours, swift-winged, unnoticed fleet;
Each tells the uncos that he sees or hears.

The parents, partial, eye their hopeful years;
Anticipation forward points the view:
The mother, wi' her needle an' her shears,
Gars auld claes look amaist as weel 's the new;
The father mixes a' wi' admonition due.

Their master's an' their mistress's command
The younkers a' are warned to obey;
An' mind their labours wi' an eydent hand,
An' ne'er, though out o' sight, to jauk or play:
"An' oh! be sure to fear the Lord alway!
An' mind your duty, duly, morn an' night!
Lest in temptation's path ye gang astray,
Implore His counsel and assisting might:
They never sought in vain that sought the Lord aright!"

But hark! a rap comes gently to the door;
Jenny, wha kens the meaning o' the same,
Tells how a neebor lad cam' o'er the moor,
To do some errands, and convoy her hame.
The wily mother sees the conscious flame
Sparkle in Jenny's e'e, and flush her cheek,
With heart-struck anxious care inquires his name,
While Jenny hafflins is afraid to speak;
Weel pleased the mother hears it 's nae wild, worthless rake.

Wi' kindly welcome Jenny brings him ben,
A strappin' youth; he taks the mother's eye;
Blythe Jenny sees the visit 's no ill ta'en;
The father cracks of horses, pleughs, and kye.
The youngster's artless heart o'erflows wi' joy,
But blate and laithfu', scarce can weel behave;
The mother, wi' a woman's wiles can spy
What makes the youth sae bashfu' an' sae grave;
Weel pleased to think her bairn's respected like the lave.

Oh, happy love! where love like this is found!
Oh, heartfelt raptures! bliss beyond compare!

I've paced much this weary mortal round,
And sage experience bids me this declare—
" If Heaven a draught of heavenly pleasure spare,
One cordial in this melancholy vale,
'Tis when a youthful, loving, modest pair
In other's arms breathe out the tender tale,
Beneath the milk-white thorn that scents the evening gale."

Is there in human form, that bears a heart—
A wretch! a villain! lost to love and truth!—
That can, with studied, sly, ensnaring art,
Betray sweet Jenny's unsuspecting youth?
Curse on his perjured arts! dissembling smooth!
Are honour, virtue, conscience, all exiled?
Is there no pity, no relenting ruth,
Points to the parents fondling o'er their child?
Then paints the ruined maid, and their distraction wild?

But now the supper crowns the simple board,
The halesome parritch, chief o' Scotia's food:
The soupe their only Hawkie does afford,
That 'yont the hallan snugly chows her cood:
The dame brings forth in complimental mood,
To grace the lad, her weel-hained kebbuck fell,
An' aft he 's prest, an' aft he ca's it gude;
The frugal wifie, garrulous, will tell,
How 'twas a towmond auld, sin' lint was i' the bell

The cheerfu' supper done, wi' serious face,
They round the ingle form a circle wide;
The sire turns o'er, wi' patriarchal grace,
The big ha' Bible, ance his father's pride:
His bonnet rev'rently is laid aside,
His lyart haffets wearing thin an' bare;
Those strains that once did sweet in Zion glide,
He wales a portion with judicious care;
And " Let us worship God!" he says, with solemn air.

They chant their artless notes in simple guise;
They tune their hearts, by far the noblest aim:
Perhaps " Dundee's" wild warbling measures rise,
Or plaintive " Martyrs," worthy of the name :
Or noble " Elgin " beets the heavenward flame,
The sweetest far of Scotia's holy lays :
Compared with these Italian trills are tame;
The tickled ears no heartfelt raptures raise;
Nae unison ha'e they with our Creator's praise.

The priest-like father reads the sacred page,
How Abram was the friend of God on high;
Or, Moses bade eternal warfare wage
With Amalek's ungracious progeny;
Or how the royal bard did groaning lie
Beneath the stroke of heaven's avenging ire;
Or, Job's pathetic plaint, and wailing cry;
Or rapt Isaiah's wild, seraphic fire;
Or other holy seers that tune the sacred lyre.

Perhaps the Christian volume is the theme,
How guiltless blood for guilty man was shed;
How He, who bore in heaven the second name,
Had not on earth whereon to lay His head:
How His first followers and servants sped;
The precepts sage they wrote to many a land:
How he, alone in Patmos banished,
Saw in the sun a mighty angel stand;
And heard great Bab'lon's doom pronounced by Heaven's
    command.

Then kneeling down, to Heaven's Eternal King,
The saint, the father, and the husband prays:
Hope " springs exulting on triumphant wing,"
That thus they all shall meet in future days:
There ever bask in uncreated rays,
No more to sigh, or shed the bitter tear,

Together hymning their Creator's praise,
In such society, yet still more dear;
While circling time moves round in an eternal sphere.

Compared with this, how poor religion's pride,
In all the pomp of method, and of art,
When men display to congregations wide,
Devotion's every grace except the heart!
The Power incensed, the pageant will desert,
The pompous strain, the sacerdotal stole;
But haply, in some cottage far apart,
May hear, well pleased, the language of the soul;
And in His book of life the inmates poor enrol.

Then homeward all take off their several way;
The youngling cottagers retire to rest:
The parent pair their secret homage pay,
And proffer up to heaven the warm request
That He who stills the raven's clamorous nest,
And decks the lily fair in flowery pride,
Would, in the way His wisdom sees the best,
For them and for their little ones provide;
But chiefly in their hearts with grace divine preside.

From scenes like these old Scotia's grandeur springs,
That makes her loved at home, revered abroad:
Princes and lords are but the breath of kings,
" An honest man's the noblest work of God:'
And certes, in fair virtue's heavenly road,
The cottage leaves the palace far behind;
What is a lordling's pomp! a cumbrous load,
Disguising oft the wretch of human kind,
Studied in arts of hell, in wickedness refined!

Oh, Scotia! my dear, my native soil!
For whom my warmest wish to heaven is sent!
Long may thy hardy sons of rustic toil
Be blest with health, and peace, and sweet content!

And, oh! may Heaven their simple lives prevent
From luxury's contagion, weak and vile!
Then, howe'er crowns and coronets be rent,
A virtuous populace may rise the while,
And stand a wall of fire around their much loved Isle.

O Thou! who poured the patriotic tide
That streamed through Wallace's undaunted heart;
Who dared to nobly stem tyrannic pride,
Or nobly die, the second glorious part,
(The patriot's God, peculiarly Thou art,
His friend, inspirer, guardian, and reward!)
Oh, never, never Scotia's realm desert;
But still the patriot, and the patriot bard,
In bright succession raise, her ornament and guard!

BLOODY DUNDEE.*

BY THE REV. J. LONGMUIR, LL.D.

A MONUMENT dazzles in brass at Auld Deer,
In the chapel where surplice and altar appear,
To the tool of the tyrant—the foe of the free,
To Claverhouse Graham—to the bloody Dundee.

Oh, *he* was the sportsman! dragoons were his dogs,
That hunted our fathers ower mountains and bogs,
Till the Bible and swords of Drumclog made him flee,
When the speed of his charger saved bloody Dundee.

But, burning with vengeance to Cov'nant and Whig,
When aided by treach'ry at Bothwell's old brig,
He butchered the swordless, no quarter gave he—
A wolf among sheep was the bloody Dundee.

* Written on hearing that "a brass" had been put up in the Episcopal Chapel, Old Deer, to the memory of "Black John of the Battles."

From the moss to his cottage he dragged godly Brown,
And scarcely allowed him in prayer to kneel down ;
But growled with an oath that he preached on his knee,—
So mad a blasphemer was bloody Dundee.

He turned to his "Satans,"—to fire gave command ;
But they drew not a trigger, they raised not a hand ;
For the prayer of the Martyr has blinded each e'e,
And they heed not the voice of the bloody Dundee.

But Claver'se his pride and his passion restrained,
While he drew forth a pistol his butcheries had stained,
And the brains of his victim soon spatter the lea,
Then away with his "lambs" rode the bloody Dundee.

Now close to their mother her infants have crept,
As she bound up the fragments, then sat down and wept,
Her wings ower her brood in their terror spread she ;
But Rinrory requited the bloody Dundee !

He tortured poor children until they revealed
The holes and the hags that their parents concealed ;
The weakness of woman enliven'd his glee,—
So kind and gallant was the bloody Dundee !

When James, as a Papist, forfaulted the throne,
IIis subjects rejoiced that the darkness had flown ;
The gleam of the Orange illumined the sea,
And brought freedom in spite of the bloody Dundee.

But Claver'se has summoned the clans from the hills,
That the Lowlands may swallow "black Prelacy's pills ;"
For claymores can teach, and the axe make you see,
That justice and truth ride with bloody Dundee !

Say, wild Killiecrankie, shall Scotland hear mass,
And Protestants pine in Dunnotar and Bass ?
No ! William approaching makes bigotry flee,
And tyranny fall with the bloody Dundee.

Then monuments garnish with thumbkin and chains,
To the man whom the blood of our Martyrs bestains;
Till Buchan's wide plains, from the hills to the sea,
Shall shudder to mouband the bloody Dundee.—*Contributed.*

SHON M'NAB.

BY ALEXANDER RODGER.

NAINSEL pe Maister Shon M'Nab,
　Pe auld 's ta forty-five, man,
And mony troll affairs she 's seen,
　Since she was born alive, man:
She 's seen the warl' turn upside down,
　Ta shentleman turn poor man,
And him was ance ta beggar loon,
　Get knocker 'pon him 's door, man.

She 's seen ta stane bow't ower ta purn,
　And syne be ca'd ta prig, man ;
She 's seen ta Whig ta Tory turn,
　Ta Tory turn ta Whig, man ;
But a' ta troll things she pe seen
　Wad teuk twa days to tell, man ;
So, gin you likes, she 'll told you shust
　Ta story 'bout hersel', man :—

Nainsel was first ta herd ta kyes
　'Pon Morven's ponny praes, man,
Whar tousand pleasant tays she 'll spent,
　Pe pu' ta nits and slaes, man ;
An' ten she 'll pe ta *herring-poat*,
　An' syne she 'll pe fish-cod, man,—
Ta place tey'll call Newfoundhims-land,
　Pe far peyont ta proad, man.

But, och-hon-ee! one misty night,
　Nainsel will lost her way, man,
Her poat was trown'd, hersel' got fright,
　She'll mind till dying day, man;
So fait! she'll pe fish-coil no more,
　But back to Morven cam', man,
An' tere she turn ta whisky still,
　Pe prew ta wee trap tram, man:

But foul pefa' ta gauger loon,
　Pe put her in ta shail, man,
Whar she wad stood for mony a tay,
　Shust 'cause she no got bail, man;
But out she'll got—nae matters hoo—
　And came to Glasgow town, man,
Whar tousand wonders *mhor* she'll saw,
　As she went up and down, man.

Ta first thing she pe wonder at,
　As she cam' down ta street, man,
Was man's pe traw ta cart himsel',
　Shust 'pon him's nain twa feet, man.
Och on! och on! her nainsel thought,
　As she wad stood and glower, man,
Puir man! if they mak you ta *horse*,
　Should gang 'pon a' your *four*, man.

And when she turned ta corner round,
　Ta black man tere she see, man,
Pe grund ta music in ta kist,
　And sell him for pawpee, man;
And aye she'll grund, and grund, and grund,
　And turn her mill about, man:
Pe strange! she will put nothing in,
　Yet aye teuk music out, man.

And when she'll saw ta peoples walk
　In crowds alang ta street, man,

She 'll wonder whar tey a' got spoons
   To sup teir pick o' meat, man ;
For in ta place whar she was porn,
   And tat right far awa, man,
Ta teil a spoon in a' ta house,
   But only ane or twa, man.

She glower to sec ta Mattams, too,
   Wi' plack clout 'pon teir face, man ;
Tey surely tid some graceless teed,
   Pe in sic black disgrace, man ;
Or else what for tey 'll hing ta clout
   Ower prow, and cheek, and chin, man,
If no for shame to show teir face,
   For some ungodly sin, man?

Pe strange to see ta wee bit kirn
   Pe jaw the waters out, man,
And ne'er rin dry, though she wad rin
   A' tay like mountain spout, man;
Pe stranger far to sec ta lamps,
   Like spunkies in a raw, man,
A' pruntin' pright for want o' oil,
   And teil a wick ava, man.

Ta Glasgow folk be unco folk,
   Ha'e tealings wi' ta teil, man,—
Wi' fire tey grund ta tait o' woo,
   Wi' fire tey card ta meal, man ;
Wi' fire tey spin, wi' fire tey weave,
   Wi' fire do ilka turn, man—
Na, some o' tem will eat ta fire,
   And no him's pelly purn, man.

Wi' fire tey mak' ta coach be rin
   Upon ta railman's raw, man ;
Nainsel will saw him teuk ta road,
   An' teil a horse to traw, man.

Anither coach to Paisley rin,
　Tey'll call him Lauchie's motion;
But oich ! she was plawn a' to bits,
　By rascal rogue M'Splosion.

Wi' fire tey mak' ta vessels rin
　Upon ta river Clyde, man,—
She saw 't hersel', as sure 's a gun,
　As she stood on ta side, man.
But gin you'll no pelieve her word,
　Gang to ta Proomielaw, man,
You'll saw ta ship wi' twa mill-wheels
　Pe grund ta water sma', man.

Oich ! sic a town as Glasgow town
　She never see pefore, man,—
Ta houses tere pe mile and mair,
　Wi' names 'poon ilka toor, man.
An' in teir muckle windows tere
　She 'll saw 't, sure 's teath, for sale, man,
Praw shentleman's pe want ta head,
　An' leddies want ta tail, man.

She wonders what ta peoples do
　Wi' a' ta braw things tere, man;
Gie her ta prose, ta kilt, an' hose,
　For tem she wadna care, man.
And aye gie her ta pickle sneesh,
　And wee drap parley pree, man;
For a' ta praws in Glasgow town
　She no gie paw-prown-pee, man.

From "Whistle Binkie," by permission of the Publisher.

A SANG O' ZION.

By George MacDonald, LL.D.

Ane by ane they gang awa ;
The gaitherer gaithers grit and sma':
Ane by ane maks ane an' a'.

Aye whan ane sets doon the cup,
Ane ahint maun tak it up;
Yet thegither they will sup.

Golden-heidit, ripe, and strang,
Shorn will be the hairst or lang:
Syne begins a better sang.

By permission of the Author.

"DOWNIE'S SLAUGHTER."

ABOUT the end of the eighteenth century, whenever any student of the Marischal College, Aberdeen, incurred the displeasure of the humbler citizens, he was assailed with the question, "Who murdered Downie?" Reply and rejoinder generally brought on a collision between "town and gown;" although the young gentlemen were accused of what was chronologically impossible. People have a right to be angry at being stigmatized as murderers, when their accusers have probability on their side; but the "taking off" of Downie occurred when the gownsmen, so maligned, were in swaddling clothes.

But there was a time, when to be branded as an accomplice in the slaughter of Richard Downie, made the blood run to the cheek of many a youth, and sent

him home to his books, thoughtful and subdued. Downie
was sacrist or janitor at Marischal College. One of his
duties consisted in securing the gate by a certain hour,
previous to which all the students had to assemble in the
common hall, where a Latin prayer was delivered by the
principal. Whether, in discharging this function, Downie
was more rigid than his predecessor in office, or whether
he became stricter in the performance of it at one time
than another, cannot now be ascertained; but there can
be no doubt that he closed the gate with austere punctu-
ality, and that those who were not in the common hall
within a minute of the prescribed time, were shut out, and
were afterwards reprimanded and fined by the principal
and professors. The students became irritated at this
strictness, and took every petty means of annoying the
sacrist; he, in his turn, applied the screw at other points
of academic routine, and a fierce war soon began to rage
between the collegians and the humble functionary.
Downie took care that in all his proceedings he kept
within the strict letter of the law; but his opponents
were not so careful, and the decisions of the rulers were
uniformly against them, and in favour of Downie. Repri-
mands and fines having failed in producing due subordin-
ation, rustication, suspension, and even the extreme
sentence of expulsion had to be put in force; and in the
end law and order prevailed. But a secret and deadly
grudge continued to be entertained against Downie.
Various schemes of revenge were thought of.

Downie was, in common with teachers and taught,
enjoying the leisure of the short New Year's vacation—
the pleasure being no doubt greatly enhanced by the
annoyances to which he had been subjected during the

recent bickerings—when, as he was one evening seated
with his family in his official residence at the gate, a
messenger informed him that a gentleman at a neighbouring hotel wished to speak with him. Downie obeyed
the summons, and was ushered from one room into
another, till at length he found himself in a large apart-
ment hung with black, and lighted by a solitary candle.
After waiting for some time in this strange place, about
fifty figures also dressed in black, and with black masks
on their faces, presented themselves. They arranged
themselves in the form of a court, and Downie, pale with
terror, was given to understand that he was about to be
put on his trial.

A judge took his seat on the bench; a clerk and public
prosecutor sat below; a jury was empanelled in front;
and witnesses and spectators stood around. Downie at
first set down the whole affair as a joke; but the proceedings were conducted with such persistent gravity,
that, in spite of himself, he began to believe in the
genuine mission of the awful tribunal. The clerk read
an indictment, charging him with conspiring against the
liberties of the students; witnesses were examined in due
form, the public prosecutor addressed the jury; and the
judge summed up.

"Gentlemen," said Downie, "the joke has been carried
far enough—it is getting late, and my wife and family
will be getting anxious about me. If I have been too
strict with you in time past I am sorry for it, and I assure
you I will take more care in the future."

"Gentlemen of the jury," said the judge, without
paying the slightest attention to this appeal, "consider
your verdict; and, if you wish to retire, do so."

The jury retired. During their absence the most profound silence was observed; and, except renewing the solitary candle that burned beside the judge, there was not the slightest movement.

The jury returned and recorded a verdict of GUILTY.

The judge solemnly assumed a huge black cap, and addressed the prisoner.

"Richard Downie! The jury have unanimously found you guilty of conspiring against the just liberty and immunities of the students of Marischal College. You have wantonly provoked and insulted those inoffensive lieges for some months, and your punishment will assuredly be condign. You must prepare for death. In fifteen minutes the sentence of the Court will be carried into effect."

The judge placed his watch on the bench. A block, an axe, and a bag of sawdust were brought into the centre of the room. A figure more terrible than any that had yet appeared came forward, and prepared to act the part of doomster.

It was now past midnight—there was no sound audible save the ominous ticking of the judge's watch. Downie became more and more alarmed.

"For any sake, gentlemen," said the terrified man, "let me home. I promise that you never again shall have cause for complaint."

"Richard Downie," remarked the judge, "you are vainly wasting the few moments that are left you on earth. You are in the hands of those who must have your life. No human power can save you. Attempt to utter one cry, and you are seized, and your doom completed before you can utter another. Every one here present has sworn a solemn oath never to reveal the proceedings of this night; they are known to none but ourselves; and when the object for which we are met is accomplished, we shall disperse unknown to any one. Prepare, then, for death; other five minutes will be allowed, but no more."

The unfortunate man, in an agony of deadly terror, raved and shrieked for mercy; but the avengers paid no heed to his cries. His fevered, trembling lips then moved as if in silent prayer; for he felt that the brief space between him and eternity was but as a few more tickings of that ominous watch.

" Now !" exclaimed the judge.

Four persons stepped forward and seized Downie, on whose features a cold clammy sweat had burst forth. They bared his neck, and made him kneel before the block.

" Strike !" exclaimed the judge.

The executioner struck the axe on the floor; an assistant on the opposite side lifted at the same moment a wet towel, and struck it across the neck of the recumbent criminal. A loud laugh announced that the joke had at last come to an end.

But Downie responded not to the uproarious merriment—they laughed again—but still he moved not—they lifted him, and Downie was dead!

Fright had killed him as effectually as if the axe of a real headsman had severed his head from his body.

It was a tragedy to all. The medical students tried to open a vein, but all was over; and the conspirators had now to bethink themselves of safety. They now in reality swore an oath among themselves; and the affrighted young men, carrying their disguises with them, left the body of Downie lying in the hotel. One of their number told the landlord that their entertainment was not yet quite over, and that they did not wish the individual that was left in the room to be disturbed for some hours. This was to give them all time to make their escape.

Next morning the body was found. Judicial inquiry was instituted, but no satisfactory result could be arrived at. The corpse of poor Downie exhibited no mark of violence internal or external. The ill-will between him and the students was known: it was also known that the students had hired apartments in the hotel for a theatrical representation—that Downie had been sent for by them; but beyond this, nothing was known. No noise had been heard, and no proof of murder could be adduced. Of two hundred students at the college, who could point out the guilty or suspected fifty? Moreover, the students were scattered over the city, and the magistrates themselves had many of their own families amongst the number, and it was not desirable to go into the affair too minutely. Downie's widow and family were provided for—and his slaughter remained a mystery; until about fifteen years after its occurrence, a gentleman on his death-bed disclosed the whole particulars, and avowed himself to have belonged to the obnoxious class of students who murdered Downie.—*From "Household Words."*

WATTY AND MEG; OR, THE WIFE REFORMED.

BY ALEXANDER WILSON.

"We dream in courtship, but in wedlock wake."—POPE.

KEEN the frosty winds were blawin',
    Deep the sna' had wreath'd the ploughs,
Watty, weary 't a' day sawin',
    Daunert down to Mungo Blew's.

Dryster Jock was sitting, crackie,
    Wi' Patie Tamson o' the hill,—
"Come awa," quo' Johnny, " Watty,
    Haith we'se ha'e anither jill."

Watty, glad to see Jock Jabos,
    And sae mony neibours roun',
Kicket frae his shoon the sna'-ba's,
    Syne ayont the fire sat down.

Ower a board wi' bannocks heapet,
    Cheese an' stowps and glasses stood;
Some were roaring, ithers sleepet,
    Ithers quietly chewt their cude.

Jock was selling Pate some tallow—
    A' the rest a racket hel',—
A' but Watty, wha, poor fellow,
    Sat and smoket by himsel'.

Mungo hil't him up a tooth-fu',
    Drank his health and Mag's in ane;
Watty, puffin out a mouthfu',
    Pledg't him wi' a dreary grane.

"What's the matter, Watty, wi' you?
  Troth your chafts are fa'in' in ;
Something's wrang—I'm vext to see you—
  Gudesake, but you're desp'rate thin!"

"Ay," quo' Watty, "things are alter't;
  But it's past redemption now,—
L—d, I wish I had been halter'd
  When I marry'd Maggy How.

"I've been poor, and vext, and raggy,
  Try't wi' troubles no that sma',—
Them I bore; but marrying Maggy
  Laid the cap-stane o' them a'.

"Night and day she's ever yelpin',
  Wi' the weans she ne'er can gree ;
When she's tir'd wi' perfect skelpin',
  Then she flees like fire on me.

"See you, Mungo, when she'll clash on
  Wi' her everlasting clack,
Whyles I've had my nieve, in passion,
  Liftet up to break her back!"

"Oh, for gudesake, keep frae cuffets!"
  Mungo shook his head and said,—
"Weel I ken what sort o' life it's;
  Ken ye, Watty, how I did?

"After Bess and I was kippl't,
  Fact, she grew like ony bear,
Brak' my shins, and, when I tippl't,
  Harl't out my verra hair!

"For a wee I quietly knuckl't;
  But when naething wad prevail,
Up my claes and cash I buckl't,—
  'Bess, for ever fare ye weel!'

" Then her din grew less and less aye,—
  Fact, I gart her change her tune ;
Now a better wife than Bessy
  Never stept in leather shoon.

" Try this, Watty—when ye see her
  Raging like a roaring flood,
Swear that moment that ye 'll lea' her;
  That 's the way to keep her gude."

Laughing, sangs, and lasses' skirls
  Echo'd now out thro' the roof.
" Done !" quo Pate, and syne his airls
  Nail't the Dryster's waukct loof.

In the thrang o' stories-telling,
  Shaking hauns, and ither cheer,
Swith ! a chap comes on the hallen,—
  " *Mungo, is our Watty here?* "

Maggie's weel-kent tongue and hurry
  Dartet thro' him like a knife.
Ope the door flew—like a fury
  In came Watty's scawlin' wife.

" Nasty, gude for naething being !
  Oh, ye snuffy, drucken sow !
Bringin' wife and weans to ruin,
  Drinkin' here wi' sic a crew !

" Devil nor your legs were broken !
  Sic a life nae flesh endures—
Toilin' like a slave to slocken
  You, ye divor, and your w——!

" Rise ! ye drucken beast o' Bethel !
  Drink's your night and day's desire;
Rise this precious hour, or faith I'll
  Fling your whisky i' the fire."

Watty heard her tongue unhallow'd,
    Pay't his groat wi' little din,
Left the house, while Maggy follow'd,
    Flyting a' the road behin'.

Fowk frae every door cam' lampin';
    Maggy curst them ane and a',
Clappit wi' her hauns, and stampin',
    Lost her bauchals i' the sna'.

Hame at length, she turn'd the gavil,
    Wi' a face as white 's a clout,
Ragin' like a verra deevil,
    Pitchin' stools and chairs about.

" Ye 'll sit wi' your limmers round you !
    Hang you, sir, I 'll be your death !
Little hauds my hauns, confound you !
    But I 'll cleave you to the teeth."

Watty, wha, 'midst this oration,
    Ey'd her whyles but daurna speak,
Sat like patient resignation,
    Trem'lin' by the ingle cheek.

Sad his wee drap brose he sippet,
    Maggy's tongue gaed like a bell,
Quietly to his bed he slippet,
    Sighin' aften to himsel':

" Nane are free frae some vexation,
    Ilk ane has his ills to dree ;
But through a' the hàle creation,
    Is a mortal vext like me ! "

A' night lang he rout and gauntet,
    Sleep nor rest he cou'dna tak' !
Maggy, aft wi' horror hauntet,
    Mum'lin', started at his back.

Soon as e'er the morning peepet,
    Up raise Watty, waefu' chiel,
Kissed his weanies, while they sleepet,
    Waukent Meg, and sought fareweel.

" Fareweel, Meg!   And oh ! may heav'n
    Keep you aye within His care ;
Watty's heart ye 've lang been grievin',
    Now he 'll never fash ye mair.

" Happy could I been beside you,
    Happy, baith at morn and e'en ;
A' the ills did e'er betide you,
    Watty aye turn't out your frien'.

" But ye ever like to see me
    Vext and sighin', late and air,
Fareweel, Meg, I 've sworn to lea' thee,
    So thou 'll never see me mair."

Meg a' sabbin' sae to lose him,
    Sic a change had never wist,
Held his haun close to her bosom,
    While her heart was like to burst.

" Oh, my Watty, will ye lea' me
    Frien'less, helpless, to despair !
Oh ! for this ae time forgi'e me,
    Never will I vex you mair."

" Aye, ! ye've aft said that, and broken
    A' your vows ten times a week :
Na, na Meg ! See there 's a token,
    Glitterin' on my bonnet cheek.

" Ower the seas I march this mornin',
    Listet, testet, sworn an' a',
Forc'd by your confounded girnin' ;
    Fareweel, Meg ! for I'm awa."

Then poor Maggy's tears and clamour
  Gusht afresh, and loudei grew,
While the weans, wi' mournfu' yammmer,
  Round their sabbin' mother flew.

"Through the yirth I'll wander wi' you—
  Stay, O Watty! stay at hame,
Here upo' my knees I'll gi'e you
  Ony vow you like to name.

"See your poor young lammies pleadin',
  Will you gang and break our heart!
No a house to put our head in!
  No a friend to tak' our part?"

Ilka word came like a bullet!
  Watty's heart begoud to shake!
On a kist he laid his wallet,
  Dightet baith his een and spake,—

"If ance mair I could, by writin',
  Lea' the sogers and stay still,
Wad ye swear to drop your flytin'?"
  "Yes, O Watty! yes I will."

"Then," quo' Watty, "mind be honest;
  Aye to keep your temper strive;
Gin ye break this dreadfu' promise,
  Never mair expect to thrive :—

"Marget How! this hour ye solemn
  Swear by everything that's gude,
Ne'er again your spouse to scol' him,
  While life warms your heart and blood, —

"That ye'll ne'er in Mungo's seek me,
  Ne'er put 'drucken' to my name,
Never out at e'ening steek me,
  Never gloom when I come hame,—

N

"That ye'll ne'er, like Bessy Miller,
  Kick my shins, and rug my hair:
Lastly, *I'm to keep the siller*—
  This upon your soul you swear?"

"O—h!" quo' Meg,—"Aweel," quo' Watty,
  "Farewcel! faith, I'll try the scas,"
"Oh, stan' still," quo' Meg, and grat aye,
  "Ony, ony way ye please."

Maggy, sync, because he prest her,
  ·Swore to a' thing ower again;
Watty lap, and danc't, and kist her;
  Wow! but he was wondrous fain.

Down he threw his staff victorious;
  Aff gaed bonnet, claes, and shoon;
Sync below the blankets, glorious,
  Held anither Hinny-Moon!

JOHN AND TIBBIE'S DISPUTE.

BY THE LATE ROBERT LEIGHTON.

JOHN DAVISON and Tibbie, his wife,
  Sat toastin' their taes ae nicht,
When something startit in the fluir,
  And blinkit by their sicht.

"Gudewife," quoth John, "did ye see that moose?
  Whar sorra was the cat?"
"A moose?"—"Ay, a moose."—"Na, na, gudeman,—
  It wasna a moose, 'twas a rat."

" Ow, ow, gudewife, to think ye 've been
    Sae lang aboot the hoose,
An' no to ken a moose frae a rat!
    Yon wasna a rat! 'twas a moose."

" I 've seen mair mice than you, gudeman—
    An' what think ye o' that?
Sae haud yer tongue an' say nae mair—
    I tell ye, it was a rat."

" *Me* haud my tongue for *you*, gudewife!
    I 'll be maister o' this hoose—
I saw 't as plain as een could see 't,
    An' I tell ye, it was a moose!"

" If you 're the maister o' the hoose,
    It 's I 'm the mistress o't;
An' *I* ken best what 's in the hoose—
    Sae I tell ye, it was a rat."

" Weel, weel, gudewife, gae mak' the brose,
    An' ca 't what ye please."
So up she rose, and made the brose,
    While John sat toastin' his taes.

They supit, and supit, and supit the brose,
    And aye their lips play'd smack;
They supit, and supit, and supit the brose,
    Till their lugs began to crack.

" Sic fules we were to fa' oot, gudewife,
    Aboot a moose"—" A what!
It 's a lee ye tell, an' I say again
    It wasna a moose, 'twas a rat!"

" Wad ye ca' me a leear to my very face?
    My faith, but ye craw croose!

I tell ye, Tib, I never will bear 't—
  'Twas a moose!"   "'Twas a rat!"   "'Twas a moose!"

Wi' her spoon she strack him ower the pow—
  " Ye dour auld doit, tak' that—
Gae to your bed, ye canker'd sumph—
  'Twas a rat!"   "'Twas a moose! '   "'Twas a rat!"

She sent the brose caup at his heels,
  As he hirpled ben the hoose;
Yet he shoved oot his head as he steekit the door,
  And cried, "'Twas a moose! 'twas a moose!"

But, when the carle was fast asleep,
  She paid him back for that,
And roar'd into his sleepin' lug,
  "'Twas a rat! 'twas a rat! 'twas a rat!"

The de'il be wi' me if I think
  It was a beast ava!
Neist mornin', as she sweepit the fluir,
  She faund wee Johnnie's ba'!

By permission of Mrs. Leighton.

MANSIE WAUCH'S FIRST AND LAST PLAY.

By D. M. MOIR, M.D.

MONY a time and often had I heard of play-acting, and of players making themselves kings and queens, and saying a great many wonderful things; but I had never before an opportunity of making myself a witness to the truth of these hearsays. So Maister Glen, being as fu' of nonsense, and as fain to have his curiosity gratified, we took upon us the stout resolution to gang ower thegither, he offering to treat me, and I determined to run the risk of Maister Wiggie our minister's rebuke, for the transgression, hoping it would make na lasting impression on his mind, being for the first and only time. Folks shouldna at a' times be ower scrupulous.

After paying our money at the door, never, while I live and breathe, will I forget what we saw and heard that night; it just looks to me, by a' the world, when I think on 't, like a fairy dream.   The place was crowded to the e'e, Maister Glen and me having nearly got our ribs dung in, before we fand a seat, and them behint were obliged to mount the back benches to get a sight.   Right to the fore hand of us was a large green curtain, some five or six ells wide, a gude deal the waur of the wear, having seen service through two or three simmers, and just in the front of it were eight or ten penny candles, stuck in a board fastened to the ground, to let us see the players' feet like, when they came on the stage, and even before they came on the stage, for, the curtain being scrimpit in length, we saw legs and feet moving behind the scenes very neatly, while twa blind fiddlers they had brought with them played the bonniest ye ever heard.   Odd, the very music was worth a sixpence of itsel'.

The place, as I said before, was choke full, just to excess, so that ane could scarcely breathe.   Indeed I never saw ony pairt sae crowded, not even at a tent-preaching, when Mr. Roarer was giving his discourses on the building of Solomon's Temple.   We were obligated to have the windows opened for a mouthful of fresh air, the barn being as close as a baker's oven, my neighbour and me fanning our red faces with our hats to keep us cool; and, though all were half stewed, we had the worst o't, the toddy we had ta'en having fomented the blood of our bodies into a perfect fever.

Just at the time that the twa blind fiddlers were playing the "Downfall of Paris," a hand-bell rang and up goes the green curtain, being hauled to the ceiling, as I observed wi' the tail o' my e'e, by a birkie at the side, that had haud o' a rope. So, on the music stopping and all becoming as still as that you might have heard a pin fall, in comes a decent old gentleman, at his leisure, weel powdered, wi' an auld-fashioned coat, and waistcoat wi' flap pockets, brown breeches with buckles at the knees, and silk stockings with red gushets on a blue ground. I never saw a man in sic distress: he stampit about, and better stampit about, dadding the end of his staff on the ground, and imploring all the powers of heaven and yearth to help him to find out his run-awa daughter, that had decampit wi' some neer-do-well loon of a halfpay captain, that keppit her in his arms frae her bedroom window, up twa pair o' stairs. Every father and head of a family maun ha'e felt for a man in his situation, thus to be robbit of his dear bairn, and an only daughter too, as he tel't us ower and ower again, as the saut saut tears ran gushing down his withered face, and he aye blew his nose on his clean callendered pocket napkin. But, ye ken, the thing was absurd to suppose that we should ken ony thing about the matter, having never seen either him or his daughter between the een afore, and no kenning them by head mark; so, though we sympathized with him, as folks ought to do with a fellow-creature in affliction, we thought it best to haud our tongues, to see what might cast up better than he expected. So out he gaed stamping at the ither side, determined, he said, to find them out, though he should follow them to the world's end, Johnny Groat's House, or something to that effect.

Hardly was his back turned, and amaist before ye could cry Jack Robison, in comes the birkie and the very young leddy the auld gentleman described, arm-and-arm thegither, smoodging and lauching like daft. Dog on it, it was a shameless piece of business. As true as death, before all the crowd of folk, he pat his arm round her waist, and caad her his sweetheart, and love, and dearie, and darling, and everything that is sweet. If they had been courting in a close thegither, on a Friday night, they couldna ha'e said mair to ane anither, or gaen greater lengths. I thought sic shame to be an e'ewitness to sic on-goings, that I was obliged at last to haud up my hat afore my face and look down, though, for a' that, the young lad, to be sic a blackguard as his conduct showed, was weel enough faured and had a guid coat on his back, wi' double-gilt buttons, and fashionable lapells, to say little o' a very weel-made pair o' buckskins, a little the waur o' the wear to be sure, but which, if they had been cleaned, would ha'e looked amaist as good as new. How they had come we never could learn, as we neither saw chaise nor gig; but, from his having spurs on his boots, it is mair than likely that they had alighted at the back door of the barn frae a horse, she riding on a pad behint him, maybe with her hand round his waist.

The faither lookit to be a rich auld bool, baith from his manner of speaking and the rewards he seemed to offer for the apprehension of his daughter; but, to be sure, when so many of us were present that had an equal

right to the spulzie, it wadna be a great deal a thousand
pounds when divided, still it was worth the looking after;
so we just bidit a wee.

Things were brought to a bearing, whosoever, sooner
than either themsel's, I daur say, or onybody else present
seemed to ha'e the least glimpse of; for, just in the middle
of their fine going-on, the sound of a coming fit was
heard, and the lassie taking guilt to her, cried out,—
" Hide me, hide me, for the sake of gudeness, for yonder
comes my auld faither!"

Nae sooner said than done. In he stappit her into a
closet; and, after shutting the door on her, he sat down
upon a chair, pretending to be asleep in a moment. The
auld faither came bouncing in, and seeing the fellow as
sound as a tap, he ran forrit, and gaed him sich a shake,
as if he wad ha'e shooken him a' sundry, which sune
made him open his een as fast as he had steekit them.
After blackguarding the chield at no allowance, cursing
him up hill and down dale, and caaing him every name
but a gentleman, he haddit his staff ower his crown, and
gripping him by the cuff o' the neck, askit him what he
had made o' his daughter. Never since I was born did
I ever see sich brazen-faced impudence! The rascal had
the brass to say at ance, that he hadna seen word or
wittens o' his daughter for a month, though mair than a
hundred folk sitting in his company had seen him dauting
her with his arm round her jimpy waist, not five minutes
before. As a man, as a father, as an elder of our kirk, my
corruption was raised, for I aye hated leeing, as a puir
cowardly sin, and an inbreak on the ten commandments:
and I fand my neebour, Mr. Glen, fidgetting on the seat
as weel as me; so I thocht, that whaever spoke first wad

ha'e the best right to be entitled to the reward; where-
upon, just as he was in the act of rising up, I took the
word out of his mouth, saying,—"Dinna believe him,
auld gentleman, dinna believe him, friend; he's telling
a parcel of lees. Never saw her for a month! It's no
worth arguing, or caaing witnesses; just open that press
door, and ye'll see whether I'm speaking truth or no."

The auld man stared, and lookit dumb-foundered;
and the young man, instead of rinning forrit wi' his
double neives to strike me, the only thing I was feared
for, began a laughing, as if I had dune him a gude turn·
But never since I had a being did I ever witness an
uproar and noise as immediately took place. The haill
house was sae glad that the scoundrel had been exposed,
that they set up siccan a roar o' lauchter, and thumpit
away at siccan a rate at the boards wi' their feet, that at
lang and last, wi' pushing, and fidgetting, and hadding
their sides, down fell the place they ca' the gallery, a' the
folk in't being hurled tapsy-turvy, head foremost amang
the saw-dust on the floor below; their guffawing sune
being turned to howling, ilka ane crying louder than
anither at the tap o' their voices,—"Murder! murder!
haud off me; murder! my ribs are in; murder! I'm
killed—I'm speechless!" and ither lamentations to that
effect; so that a rush to the door took place, in which
everything was overturned—the door-keeper being wheeled
away like wildfire—the firms strampit to pieces—the
lights knockit out—and the twa blind fiddlers dung
head foremost ower the stage, the bass fiddle cracking
like thunder at every bruise. Siccan tearing, and swearing, and tumbling, and squeeling, was never witnessed in
the memory of man, sin' the building of Babel; legs

being likely to be broken, sides staved in, een knocked out, and lives lost; there being only ae door, and that a sma' ane: so that when we had been carried off our feet that length, my wind was fairly gane, and a sick dwam cam' ower me, lights of a' manner of colours, red, blue, green, and orange dancing before me, that entirely deprived me o' common sense, till, on opening my een in the dark, I fand mysel' leaning wi' my braid side against the wa' on the opposite side of the close. It was some time before I mindit what had happened; so, dreading scaith, I fand first the ae arm, and then the ither, to see if they were broken—syne my head—and syne baith o' my legs; but a', as weel as I could discover, was skinhale and scart free. On perceiving which, my joy was without bounds, having a great notion that I had been killed on the spot. So I reached round my hand, very thankfully, to tak' out my pocket-napkin, to gi'e my brow a wipe, when lo, and behold, the tail of my Sunday's coat was fairly aff and away, dockit by the haunch buttons!

THE MITHERLESS BAIRN.

By William Thom.

When a' ither bairnies are hush'd to their hame,
By aunty, or cousin, or frecky grand-dame,
Wha stands last an' lanely, an' sairly forfairn?
'Tis the puir dowie laddie—the mitherless bairn!

The mitherless bairnie creeps to his lane bed,
Nane covers his cauld back, or haps his bare head;
His wee hackit heelies are hard as the airn,
An' lithless the lair o' the mitherless bairn!

Aneath his cauld brow, siccan dreams hover there,
O' hands that wont kindly to kaim his dark hair!
But mornin' brings clutches, a' reckless an' stern,
That lo'e na the locks o' the mitherless bairn !

The sister wha sang o'er his saftly rock'd bed,
Now rests in the mools where their mammie is laid ;
While the father toils sair, his wee bannock to earn,
An' kens na the wrangs o' his mitherless bairn.

Her spirit that pass'd in yon hour of his birth
Still watches his lone lorn wand'rings on earth,
Recording in heaven the blessings they earn,
Wha couthilie deal wi' the mitherless bairn !

Oh ! speak him na harshly—he trembles the while,
He bends to your bidding, and blesses your smile :—
In their dark hour o' anguish, the heartless shall learn,
That God deals the blow for the mitherless bairn !

THE LYART AN' LEAL.

BY JOHN CRAWFORD.

'GUDEMAN," quo' the wifie, "the cauld sough blaws eerie,
Gae steek ye the winnock, for danger I dree ;
The bluidhounds o' Clavers, forebodin' an' dreary,
I 've heard on the blast ower the snaw-covered lea—
A stranger I 've seen through the dusk o' the gloamin',
Uncovert I saw the auld wanderer kneel ;
My heart fill'd, as waefu' I heard him bemoanin'
The cauld thrawart fate o' the lyart an' leal."

The bleeze frae the ingle rose sparklin' an' cantie,
The clean aiken buffet was set on the floor ;
She thoughtna her ark o' the needfu' was scanty,
But sigh'd for the wanderer she saw on the moor.

"Ah! wae for the land whar the cauld cliffs maun shelter
The warm heart that wishes our puir kintra weel:
In thy bluid, bonny Scotland, the tyrant maun welter,
The faggot maun bleeze roun' the lyart and leal."

The tear ower her cheek row'd—the aumry stood open—
She laid out her sma' store wi' sorrowfu' heart—
The gudeman a grace ower the mercies had spoken,
Whan a tirl at the door made the kin' wifie start.
"I 'm weary," a voice cried, " I 'm hameless and harmless,
The cauld wintry blast, oh! how keenly I feel—
I 'm guiltless, I 'm guileless, I 'm friendless, an' bairnless,
Nae bluid 's on my hands," quo' the lyart an' leal.

"Ye 're welcome, auld carle, come ben to the ingle,
For snell has the blast been, an' cauld ye maun be;
In the snaw-drift sae helpless ye gar'd my heart dinnel—
Ye 'll share our puir comforts, tho' scanty they be.
A warm sowp I 've made you, expectin' your comin',
Like you, for the waes o' puir Scotland we feel;
But death soon will end a' our wailin' an' moanin',
An' youth come again to the lyart and leal."

She dichted a seat for the way-wearit stranger,
An' smilin' he sat himsel' down by the hearth—
"The Man wha our sins bore was laid in a manger,
Nae prelate proclaim'd the mild innocent's birth."
Thus spak' the auld wanderer, his een glist'n't wildly,
A sigh then escap'd for the cause he lo'ed weel;
The wifie drew closer, and spak' to him mildly,
But breathless an' cauld was the lyart an' leal.

From " Whistle Binkie," by permission of the Publisher.

BY THE ALMA: AFTER THE BATTLE.

By John Dawson.

You have found me out at last, Will; sit down beside me here,
It is not quite so hard to die when one we love is near.
You and I have known each other since we ran about the glen,
When as boys we played at soldiers, and wished that we were men.

But hark! I hear the roll of drums; and at the stirring sound
The Angel of the Battle throws his dusky wings around.
I must tell you of the battle! though my breath is failing fast,
For within my dying spirit sweeps the rousing battle blast.

Well, we scrambled through the vineyards, and we swam across the
    stream,
Above, from out the batteries' smoke, we saw the lightnings gleam.
A few fell by the river, but we reached the further banks;
And there we halted for a space, to form our broken ranks.
Sir Colin passed along our line—our grand old Highland chief;
He spoke—his words were few and stern, all soldier-like and brief:—
"Now, kilties, make me proud of this, my Highland-plumed
    Brigade;
We are going into battle, but let no one be afraid.
Don't stay to tend the wounded: if any man shall shirk,
I'll have his vile name placarded upon his parish kirk." *
"His parish kirk!"—at these two words the grim heights passed
    away,
And there in all its quiet peace our little village lay.
There was the well-known street, and there the kirk upon the hill,
With the lowly graves of the loved and lost around it calm and still.

---

* "No soldier must go carrying off wounded men. If any soldier does such a
thing, his name shall be stuck up in his parish church. Now, men, the army will
watch us; make me proud of the Highland Brigade."—Sir Colin Campbell's
Address to his Soldiers.—Kinglake's *History of the Crimea*, vol. ii., p. 450.

That sight we ne'er may see again!   There rose a smothered sob,
Along the line there seemed to pass a deep and passionate
    throb
Of eager yearning for the strife; each heart was all aflame
With courage high, to fight or die, for the dear land at " hame."

We moved a little forward, then again against our will
We had to halt; and all this while the Russians on the hill
For us had true and deadly aim; each volley left its track;
And one, faint-hearted, shouted that we might or must fall back.
Sir Colin heard the coward cry, and quick and fiery-souled,
Iis pride flamed into fury; his voice like thunder rolled,
As to the cry he answer sent—a loud and thundering "No!
Better that every man should be upon the dust laid low
Than that they now should turn their backs to the proud exulting
    foe!"

Still for a space we halted, still about the bullets flew,
And ever as the moments fled our wild impatience grew.

At last the word was spoken, the long looked-for signal made,
" Forward, Forty-second!" was all Sir Colin said,
While the visage of the veteran wore that strange and living light
Which bespeaks the soldier's rapture at the coming of the fight.

As a steed bounds with his rider when at last he has got rein;
As a stemmed-up river rushes when it bursts toward the main;
As flies the unleashed hound, or as escapes a caged bird,—
So " the Forty-second" bounded when it heard its leader's word.

Oh, Will, it is a splendid sight, a plumed and plaided host!
'Tis beautiful at home in peace; but its grandeur shines the most
When, as then, in all the glory of its martial ardour dressed,
All swift and silent at the foe " the Forty-second" pressed.

Our chieftain half-restrained us, our headlong valour stayed,
Till we march'd as firmly as we'd march at home when on parade.

On in a grand unbending line the plumes and tartan swept;
The bullets fell like hail but still our stately step we kept;
There, where we felt the fiery breath o' the red-lipped Russian gun,
The deep tramp of a thousand men was as the tramp of one.

Before us loom'd the foemen mass'd in *columns* dense and deep:
In thin and slender British *line* we climbed that deadly steep
As if it were some Highland hill our kilted lads upsprung,
While Victory like an eagle poised between the armies hung.
But Victory favoured not the dense battalions of the Russ,
For soon we saw her gracious wings would rest that day with us,
Before our fire the columns dense began to thin and sway
Till with a groan, a wailing moan, they scattered in dismay.*
Then we watched our brave Sir Colin, and we saw a signal given,
And from all along our slender line a shout went up to heaven—
That shout which comes from free-born breasts which foemen dread to
    hear,
And the Russian eagles vanished at a genuine British cheer.

     •   •   •   •   •   •

Ah, war! it is a glorious thing! but a deadly thing as well!
One face it wears is bright as heaven, and one is dark as hell.
Deep wailing from full many a home of Russian, Frank, and Turk,
And in England many tears shall be the fruit of this day's work.

Ah, me! my pulse beats faintly—quicker, quicker comes my breath,
And chill and damp my forehead feels—damp with the dews of
    death;
Draw closer to my side, dear Will, and bend thine ear this way,
While I send by thee my last farewell to dear ones far away.

My father!—when you tell him that I lie by Alma's steep,
His brow may be a shade more sad—I know he will not weep,
Unlike his son, my sire is cast in nature's sterner mould,
I often fear'd he thought me weak,—I sometimes thought him cold.

* " Then again was heard the sorrowful wail that bursts from the hearts of the brave Russian infantry when they have to suffer defeat."—Kinglake's *Crimea*, vol. ii., p. 492.

Yet I admire my noble sire, he is so true, though stern;
And if indeed, he thought me weak, he yet may live to learn
That the heart that kindles warm and bright by the fireside's kindly
    glow,
May stand like a wall of adamant in presence of the foe.
So, when you tell him that I lie here by the Alma's side,
Tell him I like a soldier fought, and like a soldier died.
Tell him—'twill give his manly heart a strange and stern delight—
That I was first across the stream, and foremost in the fight—
That, though my mortal wound I got, so early in the day,
I stemm'd it up and would not yield, but struggled through the fray.

My mother!—would that I could bear her sorrow and sharp pain.
She'll dream at night that in the fight she sees her soldier slain.
She'll wake ere morn with heavy heart her sorrow to renew—
Suppress'd by day, her tears shall fall at evening like the dew.
But tell her to control her grief, to wipe away her tears,
When the joy-bells ring for victory, and the air is rent with cheers—
When Old Scotland, 'mid her mourning for the wounded and the
    dead,
With calm and grand, yet tearful eyes, in pride uplifts her head,
That the Lion in her son's red blood yet swift to battle leapt,
And that through the long and peaceful years he was not dead, but
    slept—
That still above her banner'd host goes Victory like a star,
And, as England's first in peaceful arts, she still is first in war.
When the cities are ablaze with joy, and pride fills every breast,
Tell mother dear to raise her cheer—be joyous as the rest.
She has a right to cheer with might for England's victory won,
For she will then have paid for it the life-blood of her son.

And all my friends and comrades—some I know will weep my fall—
Tell them I ne'er forgot them—give my kindest love to all.
But deeper grows the twilight, slowly sinks the dying day.
I think I now have almost done.   Farewell, dear Will;—but stay,
There is a maid—nay, not a maid, for she is now a wife—
Whom I have told you that I loved—loved better than my life.
Her heart she said she gave me, but her hand she gave another;
I ran away, I could not stay—my rival was my brother.

Love gifts had passed between us: when I found she proved untrue
I tore her image from my heart, her gifts I from me threw.
Her image! nay, it lingers in a corner of my heart.
Her gifts!—there was a little one with which I could not part—
It was the first she gave me—a handkerchief, all hemm'd
With her own hand. This deadly day my life-blood it has stemm'd.
When, all blushing like incarnate Truth, she gave it me, I swore
That ere it and I were sunder'd 'twould be stain'd with my heart's
    gore.
So give her this, just as it is, like her 't has changed its hue
But it will tell the faithless one that I was ever true.
Nay, give me back the ghastly gift; it has too much a taint
Of vengeance : at the sight of blood her little soul would faint.
And vengeance ill becometh one who hath short time to live;
So tell her, though I ne'er forgot, I freely can forgive.

.   .   .   .   .   .

There, Will! with all things under heaven I now am almost done;
The silver cord is almost snapp'd, life's sands are all but run.
Sing to me "Auld Lang Syne," and then repeat that sweet old Psalm
You and I once learned together in the Sabbath evening's calm.

Copyright.

ENGLAND *versus* SCOTLAND:

A NIGHT AT KIRSTY CAMPBELL'S.[*]

BY ALEXANDER MACDONALD.

"DOES anybody," said the Moderator, "know where the beadle is?"

"Ou ay," replied some one, "he's ower wi' the ruling elder, Mr. Quaighhorn, ha'eing twa-three gills at Kirsty Campbell's."

Kirsty's "public" was only a stone's throw from the

[*] From *Clerical Intrigue and Counterplot:* Cameron & Ferguson, Glasgow and London.

O

kirk, and the beadle, Donald M'Wheesht, was accordingly sent for, as the Moderator intimated that the proceedings must be stopped until there was some one in attendance to see that order was kept.

Donald was uncommonly fond of a "tram" at all times—never so much so, however, as when he succeeded in getting it "frae a freen," and he was now in that state which is sufficiently understood by the comparatively mild expression, "powerfully refreshed." Like a good many people in that happy condition, he fancied that nobody could for a moment imagine that he was not perfectly fit for business; but he unfortunately lost his balance in trying to be too *nonchalant*, by wishing to insert his snuff-spoon into his mull to take a more deliberate pinch, when he might have successfully accomplished that delicate operation by the use of his finger and thumb.

"Where have you been?" sternly demanded the Moderator, rising from his seat and fixing M'Wheesht, as his snuff-spoon every now and then missed the mouth of the crooked mull, much as provoking watch keys will persist in dodging holes in the hands of some individuals at that indefinite hour when it is said to be all one after twelve.

"Where have you been?" again exclaimed the Moderator.

"Oot bye," answered Donald.

"Were you drinking in Kirsty Campbell's, sir?"

"Maybe ay and maybe no," complacently replied the beadle; and looking round the church with a drunken leer, he slowly ejaculated,—

"Ye 've been gey an' aften there yersel'!"

"Take the fellow out, he 's a drunkard and liar!" exclaimed the Moderator, reddening like a turkey-cock; and sitting down, he was obliged to say,—

" We must do without him. Go on, Mr. Garrempey."

Donald gave a hiccupy laugh, and staggered out of the church, to rejoin his friends at Kirsty's.

Garrempey, on getting out of the close and fetid atmosphere of the church, was strongly tempted to adjourn to Kirsty Campbell's "public," if he could only fall in with some congenial soul, to keep him company, for, with all his failings, he never drank alone. As luck would have it, his wandering eye lighted upon the slim and elegant figure of Mr. Charles Edward Puff, who was generally supposed to be the Paris correspondent of the London Daily *Flabbergaster.*

Charley had made rapid progress in his Scottish education. He had become quite as good a judge—and quite as efficient a drinker of the various Scotch whiskies as the redoubtable Huistan himself, a feat which it had been the height of his ambition to accomplish; for it seems to be part of the instinct of an Englishman— particularly of a Cockney—to stop short at nothing to equal a Scotsman; if possible, to beat him in his own country, whether, by so doing, he makes himself ridiculous or not.

Charley, besides, had fairly won the admiration of Huistan, not merely by his prowess as a drinker, but by having actually got the better of that astute individual in a desperate dispute with regard to the purity of his own Gaelic.

" Let's go," he said, "and see how Kirsty's getting on. A tumbler of that cool water 'frae the wall,' with a cinder in it, would go down amazingly just now."

"Agreed. I feel almost inclined to make a night of it here, instead of going all the way to Porterbier. I'm quite fagged and worn out."

"I'm your man, then; come! cheer up, Gabby, you'll beat these fellows yet, if there's law or common sense left in broad Scotland."

Garrempey shook his head, as they entered Kirsty's sanded parlour. "You don't know the outs and ins of an ecclesiastical case so well as I do, Charley, or you would know that it's a mere toss up in the Assembly."

"Well, we aren't much better off at home, although certainly we haven't this precise way of doing things. Don't let the thoughts of it spoil your appetite, however," continued the lively Englishman, as they sat down to the tempting black-faced mutton chops which Charley had ordered to be ready at a previous visit to the "public."

"Hallo! here's our friend Huistan," he exclaimed, in the same cheery mood. "Come in, my worthy son of Fingal, chief of lifters, we're going to have a chop, and make a night of it under the shade of the Auld Kirk! What do you say to that Hugh?"—giving him a hearty thump upon his broad back.

"A' richt, Chairley, but ye'll maybe ken the auld freat, 'The nearer the kirk, the farther frae grace.'"

"Can't be much nearer the last article, Hugh, than we are now," said Charley, at once beginning with "For what we are going to receive,"—

"Man, ye're an awfu' heathan, Chairley!" said Huistan, when he had finished, with a look, as to which it would be difficult to say whether it was more indicative of the chuckle or the frown.

"You English care nae mair for spiritu"—
"Don't say that, now, Hugh. Just ask my purse or the stocking in which you keep your bank account. Either of them will tell you that I've invested pretty extensively in the spirit trade."

"Hear till him noo!" said Huistan, fairly in for a hearty laugh.

"Come along, Gabby! mix up," called out Charley, after the cloth had been removed and the "ammunition" had been brought in. "Huistan's just clearing his tunnel for the usual overture, ' Ta praise o' Whuskey.'"

"TA PRAISE O' WHUSKEY."

Air—*Neil Gow's Farewell to Whiskey.*

Ta praise o' whuskey she will kive,
An' wish ta glaiss aye in her neive,
She disna' socht that she could live,
    Wisoot a wee drap whuskey, O!

For whuskey is ta sing ma laad,
Tae cheer her heart whane'er she's saad,
An' trive bad sochts awa like mad,
    Pheugh! tere's naething like goot whuskey, O!

O! whuskey's goot, an whuskey's gran',
Ta pestest pheesic efer fan',
She wishes she had in her han',
    A great pig shar o' whuskey, O!

Ta leddies tey will glower an' blink,
Whane'er tey'll saw't a man in trink,
Put by themsel' tey'll nefer wink,
    At four pig trams o' whuskey, O!

Garrempey began at last to wake up, and song and toast and brimming glass succeeded each other, as only these highly disciplined bacchanalians could make them do. By a curious psychological phenomenon, which can never probably be satisfactorily accounted for, everything seemed to go on smoothly, during these jolly *noctes*, until the mixing of the fifth tumbler, but the moment Charley felt a devilish inclination to pitch into the Scotch, that moment he knew that he was drinking genuine Ardbeg, and that he was, to a certainty, beginning his fifth tumbler.

"Yes," he said, with an unmistakable sneer, after having been engaged for some minutes in looking intently into his tumbler.

"Yes, you're a peculiar people, you Scotch—you are —Hang me! if it's possible to live with you anywhere in comfort! You must quarrel with somebody rather than be idle. Your cursed industry must find employment, even in pulling to pieces the Auld Kirk itself."

"Ye sud ha'e sed, at the door o' ma whuskey shop at ance, Maister Chairles, for I ken brawly that's what ye're meanin'," exclaimed Huistan, whose *birse* was beginning to rise.

"Dear me! Mr. M'Huistan," replied Charley, also standing upon his dignity, and putting off reluctantly a malicious inclination to make matters worse.

"Dear me, what's your dander up for now?"

"It's too grave a maitter," said Huistan, unwittingly perpetrating a pun, "to be treated in that way."

"Well, well, Mr. M'Huistan, if we've been ill-treating any subject, we have been maltreating ourselves at the same time. Let it be like tales that ne'er were told.

Here's tae a' *honest* Scotchmen.'" He emphasied "honest."

"Meanin' oor absent freens, I reckon," said Huistan, now fairly roused. "I ken your meanin' be yer mumpin'. I'll no drink 't."

"Well, then, you may be ——"

"No, I'll no be ——"

"What the deuce is all this about?" suddenly exclaimed Garrempey, who had been roused from his slumber by the noisy voices of his excited companions.

"Aboot?" said Huistan; "ye may weel ask that. It's Maister Chairles there, takin' advantage o' me because ye're asleep, an' abuisin' oor country, as he kent weel that I wasna' sae able as ye are tae tackle him."

"Oh! indeed," said Garrempey, "at his old tricks again? What's the grievance now? Is it the lion and the unicorn again, or the Wallace monument, or have they given any other government appointment to a Scotchman?"

"Ou, he's jist been saying, wi' ane o' thae infernal sneers o' his, that we're a pecooliar people, an has been likening us tae Kilkenny cats, and Gude kens what."

"Well, if we're a peculiar people, I suppose you'll admit, Charley, that we're also zealous of good works?" said Garrempey, in his usual quiet way.

"I don't deny your zeal, you have taken sufficient pains to let the world know all about it, and to flaunt before us, what you call the *perfervidum ingenium Scotorum;* but I say again, you're prudish, narrow-minded, clannish, and given over to the most zealous cultivation of trifles."

"Oh, ho!" said Garrempey, scenting like the war horse the battle, but not from afar.

"What precise charge do you make against us now, Mr. Puff?"

"Why, there's that absurd movement the other day, of your restless professor of Greek in Edinburgh—Blackie, and some of his congeners, heralded by a petition to the Queen, to compel us in England to call everything British instead of English—British press, British army, British Parliament. There'll be nothing left of old England at all, if these fellows have their way of it. The roast beef of old England must become the roast beef of old Britain. We shall have to get new editions of all our standard works, expunging every allusion to England. Let's see how it would go. We'll take 'Ye Mariners of England.'"

"Campbell," growled forth Garrempey.

"Yes, Campbell," regrowled Charley. "What of that?"

"Old England," cynically, replied Garrempey.

"Old dot—"—but Charley checked himself, and began to sing with a ludicrously correct imitation of the mode in which Huistan would certainly have sung that song—

"Ye ma-a-rinars of Bree-ee-tan."

"Tam it! Maister Chairles, are ye mockin' me?"

"Not at all, Mr. M'Huistan. I'm merely trying to see how the song would answer to the new regulations proposed by Professor Blackie. We would require, I'm afraid, to ask that highly respectable and restless professor to remodel our prosody for us, which, of course, he would be very willing to do. I've no doubt he would also propose that we should read English with a strong Caledonian accent, just as he is now making his unfortunate students do with Homer, by getting them to read the immortal lines of the great bard, as if he had spoken a bastard dialect of Byzantine Greek, instead of Ionian."

(They were now at their seventh tumbler.)'

"It's a great pity, Mr. Garrempey," said Charley, "that Sydney Smith hadn't been a Scotchman. In that case he would certainly have got an appointment."

"In *partibus infidelium*, I dare say."

"No, sir; in the parts which have been assigned to the Archbishop of Canterbury."

"Indeed. You don't happen to be aware, Mr. Puff, do you, of the precise reason which induced Mr. Disraeli to make that appointment?"

"Because Dr. Tait was a Scotchman, of course."

"Don't you believe it, sir. Mr. Disraeli has no love for the Scotch, for two reasons: first, because he can't humbug them as he can the Buckinghamshire farmers and the old nobility, and—"

"I dare say not. One Jew doesn't generally try it on with another."

"Thank you; we shall let that pass just now. The second is, that the Scotch have done more harm to the Conservative cause than either your countrymen or the Irish. Knowing—for what is it that Disraeli doesn't know?—that the old stock of grievances and invective was about worn out, he resolved to play a bold card—as he generally does—to cap the list, in fact, by giving the Archbishop's hat to Dr. Tait."

"Very unfair to Mr. Disraeli, sir. I have no doubt his real motive was, that as the Church of England possesses a somewhat exuberant udder, and more than one teat, it would only be an act of charity to let one of them be sucked by a Scotchman."

" Weel, I declare! Mr. Garrempey," said Huistan, who had nearly lost his breath, " that coo's the gowan! I doot he's got us noo."

" Let us be thankful, Huistan, he didn't say that the Scotchman, having got hold of one teat, would be certain to have the udder too."

" Well, if I didn't say it, I at least thought it.   If things are to be called English, why, they *will* be called English, in spite of all you can do or say to the contrary.   Just as surely as the English will eat up your Gaelic—"

" Got! I railly believe they wud eat up onything; put Got forbid!" said Huistan, with pious horror " that they sud devoor the Gaalic—that wud be maist onnaitral, an' in fac' onreesonable."

" And highly indigestible, too," said Charley, fairly forced into good humour by the seriousness which his last speech had produced in Huistan's face, but particularly as the eighth tumbler had now come into play, which, failing the seventh, usually put matters all straight.

SANDY M'TEEVISH *versus* JOHN BULL:
A Few Words About the Union.*

By Alexander Macdonald.

"Well, you must admit, Charley," said Garrempey, "that it's most unfair of you to break the faith of Treaties?"

" Bah!   Treaties are like pie crust, made to be broken. You can't legislate for posterity, except for the one or two generations you can yourself hold in leading strings.

* From *Clerical Intrigue and Counterplot:* Cameron & Ferguson, Glasgow and London.

You can't mortgage, by Treaties, the wills and dispositions of the millions that are to be born some two or three hundred years hence."

" No; but you can set them a good example."

" We set them the best example we can. We give fair play to the course of events. We neither force on, nor retard the progress of ideas, nor attempt to lead the fashions of speech any more than those of dress. If it was part of a Treaty of Union, made a hundred and fifty years ago, that a cap was to be eternally called a *mutch*, for the gratification of the Scotch, do you suppose we could prevent the ladies now-a-days from calling it a bonnet if they chose?"

" Then you admit that you have broken the Treaty of Union ?"

" I admit nothing without proof and argument. You have not satisfied me that you are right in your contention."

" Well, then," said Garrempey, having seen that his tumbler was well and duly replenished, " once for all, let me state the case for the Plaintiff."

" Go it, Gabby! Huistan, call the case Sandy M'Teevish *versus* John Bull."

" A' richt Chairley. O, yes! O, yes! an' anither O, yes! That's three ca's."

" Now Gabby, since Huistan has called the roll, open your ports for action, but avoid personalities."

" No fear, Charley; I mean to fight hard, but I'll fight fair. Now, how stands the case? You will, of course, admit the patent fact, that rather better than one hundred and fifty years ago, John Bull and Sandy M'Teevish considered it to be for their mutual advantage to enter into a Treaty of Union?"

"Did they, railly?" earnestly inquired Huistan, whose intellect was not exactly in its sharpest state just at that particular stage of the evening.

"*Heus tu! mon enfant, taisez vous*, and let Gabby go on," said Charley, now in what Garrempey called his daftest mood.

"What's that ye're sayin', Chairley, aboot teazin'? I dinna' onderstaun' yer' Greek an' Laitin."

"A Treaty of Union," solemnly continued Garrempey, "in other words, a contract of copartnery, by which they settled their mutual interests. It was expressly covenanted that the firm thereby constituted, was to be known to all whom it might concern, as the firm of BULL AND M'TEEVISH. Under this *nomen socii* the company carried on its business, and has prospered. M'Teevish has contributed, in proportion to his interest, as much, if not more capital than Bull, and bears, at least, a proportional share of the working expenses."

"I deny that, Gabby."

"Wheesht noo, Chairley! ye ken ye stoppit me," interposed Huistan.

"His sons," continued Garrempey, with some emotion, "have shed their best blood fully and freely upon many a hard-fought field, and under many a burning sun, for the protection and profit of the old concern."

Here Huistan became visibly affected, and Charley was seen to wink twice.

"And," continued Garrempey, not unobservant of the impression which he had just made, "to a very considerable extent they have allowed the sons of John to enjoy the congenial indulgence of sitting at home at ease."

"Hold hard, Gabby. I can't admit—"

"Is he bringin't hame tae the faimily, Chairley?"

"Peace, Hugh! Go on, Gabby. I promise I won't stop you again."

"They have done," resumed the speaker, "very much to give stability, as colonists, to the possessions of the firm in foreign parts, and, in fact, they are remarkable for being no where so much at home as when they are abroad."

"Or in England," added Charley, mechanically, and evidently forgetful of his promise.

"But in recent times," continued Garrempey, "John seems to take it for granted that, because he is senior partner and cashier, and encases himself in breeches somewhat wider round the abdomen than those of his partner, he can, with propriety, ignore his existence. He thinks it is more convenient, and probably more euphonious, to call the offices of the company, Bull's chambers, and the vessels, Bull's ships, but I think it is not generous nor fair of John to feel ashamed of the partner who has worked with him so long, and attempt to avoid performance of his social duties, by trite jokes and flimsy arguments."

"Well, Gabby, you have stated the case for the Plaintiff 'no that bad,' to repeat the whisper which I couldn't help hearing, of your able junior; but without entering at present into the case for the defence, permit me just to ask you this. You say that the term 'English' is wrong, and that it should be 'British.' What, then, are we to do with the Irish?"

"The Eerish?" said Huistan. "Ye needna' be muckle fashed wi' them, Chairley, for I'm sure ye telt me mony a time, that the only wey tae deal wi' them, was jist tae gie Heebernia, as ye ca'd her, a bit dook in the Atlantick."

" That was to get quit of the Fenians, Hugh."

" Ou ay," said Huistan, " I see."

" You know, Gabby," continued Charley, " that the three kingdoms are called the United Kingdom of Great Britain and Ireland. According to your theory, if we are to call everything British, we will, of course, exclude Ireland altogether, and you may depend upon it, that if we did so, we should have another question as difficult as that of the Irish Church. That would never do. What would THE O'DONOGHUE say to it?"

" May I answer that question, *more Scotorum*, by putting another?"

" *More Scotorum*, Gabby, I don't know whether you are better at putting questions or begging them, but you can take the matter to avizandum, as your judges say, when they have already made up their minds what their judgment is to be. Proceed."

" You are doubtless aware," resumed Garrempey, "that Canada, Australia, and New Zealand are British possessions, in the precise sense in which West India plantations may be the property of Smith and Jones. They are held for behoof of the firm. Scotland, with regard to England, is in the position of one *qui rem aliquem cum alio possidet*, and although these Colonies are part of the property of the State, they are not the State itself, any more than the joint possession of a coffee plantation would make it the firm of Smith and Jones. · I don't suppose the eminent Smith would experience any difficulty in doing the right thing, by calling his firm by its proper name, because the company owned large pos-

sessions in Jamaica. Such an *embarras de richesses*
would not turn his practical head; but if he were a funny
man, like Bull, he might probably try to laugh his partner
into sinking his *nomen socii*, by comic allusions to the
quality of leeks, and facetious doubts as to the existence
of Caractacus, and the genealogy of Cadwallader."

"Anything else, Gabby?" asked Charley, with a
peculiarity of utterance, and with a look which betrayed
the fact that he had been paying more attention to some
other matter than to Garrempey's discourse. That
gentleman was, however, so much absorbed in his argument, the thread of which he never for a moment lost,
that he did not notice that he was two tumblers behind
his two cronies; for, although Huistan had religiously
filled his glass each time he and Charley helped themselves, and poured it into his tumbler, Garrempey having
the feeling strong upon him that he was pleading a *bona
fide* legal case, relied mechanically more upon his snuff
than upon his toddy. The consequence was that at this
particular stage of the proceedings, he had about two
glasses and a half of whisky in his tumbler, with only as
much water as served to melt the load of sugar which
had been accumulated by Huistan's faithful performance
of his duty.

He felt somewhat nettled at the curt inquiry made by
Charley, as to whether he had anything else to say, and
it stopped him for a moment. It was a critical moment,
for he had been gathering himself up for a great effort, a
crushing peroration which would have crowned the argument he had been so industriously rearing in support of
the rights of his country. Somewhat hastily and excitedly
seizing his tumbler without suspecting that he had fallen

into arrear, he swallowed its contents almost at a gulp. Fatal draught! It will rob him of the triumph of which he was all but certain. See! he is conscious of his error. He feels the subtle poison hastening to occupy his brain! He knows his danger, and he makes a supreme effort—concentrating all the powers of his mind upon the accomplishment of the momentous issue.

With a look of dogged resolve he proceeds,—

" Everybody knows that New England, although one of the States, is not the United States of America any more than old England is the United Kingdom. If nationality is to be sunk by an agglomeration of races it should be sunk by all. We Scotsmen," he exclaimed, looking proudly around, " are content to sink it with England, but not without her. With her we consent to be British, but with her or without her we will *not* be English. No man loves an Englishman more than I do. I believe he furnishes as fair a test of all that is manly and honourable as it is necessary to seek for, but I am not disposed to be called the Englishman I am not, and cease to be the Scotsman I am, to humour a fashion, or avert a sneer. Above all, I am not willing to carry about with me the ugly feeling of being merely the hybrid descendant of an inferior and conquered race!"

" Bravo! Gabby—God bless you, my boy!" was all, alas! that Charley was able to articulate, and that by no means distinctly.

" Got pless us a' three baith thegeither!" mumbled poor Huistan, while both Charley and he, by a miracle, managed to attain what the latter called their *equalbill-arum*.

Garrempey got up at the same time.

But he, too, like his friends, was obliged to succumb to the victorious Ardbeg. The three worthies were found by Kirsty at a nameless hour in the morning—standing upright, it is true, but in a position which looked as if they had succeeded in improvising themselves into a temporary theodolite, or had accomplished the interesting operation of piling arms. They were *Tres in uno.* The Treaty of Union was again complete. May it ever remain so!

LOCHINVAR.

BY SIR WALTER SCOTT, BART.

OH, young Lochinvar is come out of the west!
Through all the wide border his steed was the best;
And save his good broad-sword, he weapon had none,
He rode all unarm'd, and he rode all alone!
So faithful in love, and so dauntless in war,
There never was knight like the young Lochinvar!

He staid not for brake, and he stopp'd not for stone,
He swam the Eske river, where ford there was none;
But, ere he alighted at Netherby gate,
The bride had consented, the gallant came late:
For a laggard in love, and a dastard in war,
Was to wed the fair Ellen of brave Lochinvar!

So boldly he enter'd the Netherby hall,
'Mong bride's men, and kinsmen, and brothers, and all!
Then spoke the bride's father, his hand on his sword—
For the poor craven bridegroom said never a word—

P

"O come ye in peace here, or come ye in war?
Or to dance at our bridal, young Lord Lochinvar?"

"I long woo'd your daughter, my suit you denied:
Love swells like the Solway, but ebbs like its tide!
And now I am come, with this lost love of mine,
To lead but one measure, drink one cup of wine!
There be maidens in Scotland, more lovely by far,
Who would gladly be bride to the young Lochinvar!"

The bride kiss'd the goblet; the knight took it up,
He quaff'd off the wine, and he threw down the cup!
She look'd down to blush, and she look'd up to sigh,
With a smile on her lips and a tear in her eye.
He took her soft hand ere her mother could bar,—
"Now tread we a measure!" said young Lochinvar.

So stately his form, and so lovely her face,
That never a hall such a galliard did grace!
While her mother did fret, and her father did fume,
And the bridegroom stood dangling his bonnet and plume,
And the bride-maidens whisper'd, "'Twere better by far,
To have match'd our fair cousin with young Lochinvar."

One touch to her hand, and one word in her ear,
When they reach'd the hall door, and the charger stood near,
So light to the croupe the fair lady he swung,
So light to the saddle before her he sprung!
"She is won! we are gone, over bank, bush, and scaur;
They'll have fleet steeds that follow!" quoth young Lochinvar.

There was mounting 'mong Græmes of the Netherby clan;
Fosters, Fenwicks, and Musgraves, they rode and they ran;
There was racing and chasing on Cannobie Lea,
But the lost bride of Netherby ne'er did they see!
So daring in love, and so dauntless in war,
Have ye e'er heard of gallant like young Lochinvar?

HAIL, LAND OF MY FATHERS!

By Professor Blackie.

Hail, land of my fathers ! I stand on thy shore,
'Neath the broad fronted blufis of thy granite once more;
Old Scotland, my mother, the rugged, the bare,
That reared me with breath of the strong mountain air.
No more shall I roam where soft indolence lies,
'Neath the cloudless repose of the featureless skies,
But where the white mist sweeps the red furrow'd scaur,
I will fight with the storm and grow strong by the war !

What boots all the blaze of the sky and the billow,
Where manhood must rot on inglorious pillow ?
'Tis the blossom that blooms from the taint of the grave,
'Tis the glitter that gildeth the bonds of the slave.
But, Scotland, stern mother, for struggle and toil
Thou trainest thy children on hard rocky soil;
And thy stiff-purposed heroes go conquering forth,
With the strength that is bred by the blasts of the north.

Hail, Scotland, my mother! and welcome the day
When again I shall brush the bright dew from the brae,
And light as a bird, give my foot to the heather,
My hand to my staff, and my face to the weather,
Then climb to the peak where the ptarmigan flies,
Or stand by the linn where the salmon will rise,
And vow never more with blind venture to roam
From the strong land that bore me—my own Scottish home.

By permission of the Author.

THE END.

BELL AND BAIN, PRINTERS, 41 MITCHELL STREET, GLASGOW.

OPINIONS OF THE PRESS.

"This volume of over 200 pages contains some of the choicest readings on Scottish subjects, in prose and verse, with which a spare half hour may be beguiled. The book is well got up—an attractive cover, good type, clear printing, and excellent paper."—*Budget.*

"Not the least interesting feature of this collection of Scottish Readings by our townsman, Mr. Mair, is the local interest that some of the pieces have, these being taken from the works of the best known of our Aberdeenshire writers. There is in this volume reproduced some of Anderson's best productions, such as, 'Jean Findlat r's Loon,' and along with several choice pieces from Thom, the weaver poet, we have the famous 'Legend of St. Swithin,' by the late George Davidson, whose death only happened a few weeks ago. This piece in itself is a sufficient attraction to the volume, but more so when there is on the cover a copy from the well known drawing by Faed of the droughty saint engaged in working his 'hellish charm.'

"The majority of the pieces brought together in this cheap form are copyrights, thus giving the volume a freshness which no other collection of the kind possesses. Although there cannot be very much originality displayed by the editor of such a book, still in this case the necessary work has been done well and to good advantage."—*Aberdeen Free Press.*

"*The Book of Scottish Readings* is a collection of stories and sketches in prose and verse. Some few of them are new, but more have already earned a good reputation. The volume is interesting and healthy in tone."—*Scotsman.*

"The editor has done his work well, and the little book before us is, in its comical readings, a refutation of the old scandal, that before you could get a joke into a Scotchman's head, it was necessary for him to submit to a surgical operation. 'There's no " wit" in Scotland,' said Sydney Smith ; 'only an inferior copy of it, called " wut."' Perhaps the Scotch may parry the attack by asserting that we English don't understand their language; at any rate, every inhabitant of 'Auld Reekie,' or 'Braid Scotland,' who wishes to disprove the above scandal, should buy this book and send it to his English friends. There are, we need not add, many pathetic readings as well."—*Publisher's Circular.*

"This excellent compilation will no doubt soon become very popular. Considering the great amount of matter ready to be laid under contribution for a work of this kind, the selections have been very judiciously made; embracing, as they do, the humorous and pathetic, the grave and the gay. Amongst the authors quoted are—Dr. George MacDonald, Professor Aytoun, Thomas Carlyle, Dr. John Brown, Professor Blackie, Rev. George

Gilfillan, Robert Chambers, Professor Wilson, James Hogg, &c. &c. Among the pieces having a local interest we may mention the 'Legend of St. Swithin,' by the late Mr. George Davidson, whose facile pen was no stranger to our readers, and 'Downie's Slaughter.' We cordially commend this compilation to the attention of our readers."—*Aberdeen Herald.*

"This is a capital compilation, by our townsman, Mr. James Allan Mair. The selections have been carefully made, and will be found admirably adapted for reading aloud in the home circle or at public entertainments. The humorous, of course, largely predominates; but there are passages from our own graver national writers descriptive of memorable events in Scottish history. The writers placed under contribution include Burns, Carlyle, George Gilfillan, Professors Blackie and Aytoun, Delta, the Ettrick Shepherd, Robert Chambers, and a host of others more or less celebrated. Among the short stories introduced, 'The Scot Abroad,' and 'A Night at Tibbie Campbell's,' are racy in the extreme, and sure to awaken uproarious mirth in a mixed audience."—*People's Journal.*

"This little volume contains some very choice readings on Scottish subjects, both in prose and verse. Unlike the very trashy stories so prevalent in these days, *Scottish Readings* are chiefly from authors of acknowledged status; and those in the Scottish dialect are good specimens of the language, both in its old and its more modern form, while in idea and expression they are well fitted to beguile a spare half-hour. The sketches are all readable—a thing which cannot be said of much that is written and printed now-a-days—and some of them are fine compositions, not easily accessible to the general reader. The book deserves a wide circulation."—*Fifeshire Advertiser.*

"This is a choice selection, thoroughly Scottish in every particular, and just the very thing for a night of Scotch readings all over the world. Within the compass of some 215 pages, the editor has given Scotchmen a treat which will be relished by every mither's son and brither Scot from Ultima Thule to the end of the earth."—*Northern Ensign.*

"This is a very attractive volume, and the contents are selected with great taste from some of the best writers of Scottish literature. There are a number of poems, stories, and sketches in English, but by far the greatest portion of the pages of the book are filled with selections which embrace specimens of the Scottish tongue in its old and also its more recent forms. The Highland, Lowland, and East Coasts dialects are well represented. Altogether the work presents in a limited space some of the choicest readings on Scottish subjects in 'prose and verse,' at which a half-hour may be pleasantly beguiled."—*The Buchan Observer.*

For the Flute.

ADAMS'S POPULAR SERIES.

THE ART OF PLAYING THE FLUTE WITH-
OUT A MASTER: an improved and complete Tutor for
the Instrument; with Instructions, Scales, and 66 Popular Airs. Price 6d., post free for 7 stamps.

100 SCOTTISH AIRS FOR THE FLUTE; with
Instructions and Scales for the Instrument. Price 6d.,
post free for 7 stamps.

**100 ENGLISH AND NATIONAL AIRS FOR
THE FLUTE;** with Instructions and Scales for the
Instrument. Price 6d., post free for 7 stamps.

100 IRISH AIRS FOR THE FLUTE; with
Instructions and Scales for the Instrument. Price 6d.,
post free for 7 stamps.

100 CHRISTY'S MINSTRELS' AIRS FOR THE
FLUTE; with Instructions and Scales for the Instrument. Price 6d., post free for 7 stamps.

THE AIRS OF ALL NATIONS FOR THE
FLUTE; containing upwards of 200 Popular Airs; with
Instructions, Scales, &c. Price 1s., post free for 13
stamps.

For the Violin.

ADAMS'S POPULAR SERIES.

THE ART OF PLAYING THE VIOLIN WITH-
OUT A MASTER: an improved and complete Tutor
for the Instrument; with Instructions, Scales, and 65
Popular Airs. Price 6d., post free for 7 stamps.

100 SCOTTISH AIRS FOR THE VIOLIN; with
Instructions and Scales for the Instrument. Price 6d.,
post free for 7 stamps.

**100 ENGLISH AND NATIONAL AIRS FOR
THE VIOLIN;** with Instructions and Scales for the
Instrument. Price 6d., post free for 7 stamps.

www.ingramcontent.com/pod-product-compliance
Lightning Source LLC
Chambersburg PA
CBHW030118030726
47498CB00007B/2436